# VERA

## SHE WHO DARES, WINS

JOANNA NIGHTINGALE

First published 2024 by Magic Daisy Publishing

www.magicdaisypublishing.co.uk

Copyright © Magic Daisy Publishing 2024
Text copyright © Joanna Nightingale 2024
Cover photography © Rev Donald McCorkindale 2024

The moral rights of the author has been asserted

All rights reserved
No part of this publication may be reproduced or transmitted by any means, electronic, mechanical, photocopying or otherwise without the prior permission of the publishers

ISBN 979-8-8717-6463-3

Printed and bound by Amazon

For my family.

# 1

Vera stood at the bow of the ferry eagerly looking for the island of Strathsay. The lighthouse and the majestic old church were the first landmarks she recognised from her research, as the ferry slowly approached the Island.

This was a completely new start. What had drawn her here so powerfully? Her lifelong dream of living in a croft had by a sheer coincidence come true. It was both exciting and at the same time very scary. A new house, a completely new way of living, far away from everybody and everything she knew. Yet it somehow felt so right that it had not taken her very long to make up her mind, when the opportunity of moving up here suddenly had presented itself only a couple of months ago, on a very ordinary Tuesday evening in December.

Big shafts of sunlight penetrated the grey clouds and danced over the island. White crofts were scattered like bits of confetti on the softly undulating green hills. Their slate roofs glittered like diamonds in the early morning sun. Which one was her new home? 'Harbour View'. *Her croft!*

Suddenly a huge rainbow appeared over the green island. This was the croft she had been dreaming of for years, and of which she had imagined every little detail in her mind. It would have a chimney at each end of the house. The wooden front door would be in the middle of the building; it had a little glass canopy over it held up by ornate cast iron brackets. (She wasn't entirely sure where she'd got that little detail from.) It had deep-set windows on either side of the door, which emphasised the solidity off the walls. It would have a pitched slate roof. The floors would be the old-fashioned reddish brown quarry tiles in the kitchen and varnished floorboards everywhere else. The walls would be white washed both inside and out. There would be wood burning stoves, so the house would be warm.

And unbelievably one of these houses up there on the hillsides would be that dream come true. She had gone outside. It was cold out on the deck, it was only very early March, so not even quite the spring equinox. The clocks would go forward to summer time at the end of the month.

The unfamiliar and slightly queasy feeling in the pit of her stomach could be due to either nervousness or slight seasickness. It was after all a life changing decision she had made. Being outside helped the unfamiliar feeling. Having the fresh cold air on her face and breathing it deep down into her lungs helped too. She could feel a gentle swell, even though the sea appeared calm. It felt particularly good that the air was so clean and fresh. What a contrast to the air on The Isle of Dogs in London, where she had lived for the last 28 years. She took slow deep breaths, filled her lungs to the brim and added a contented little noise of mmmm as she slowly let it go again. The breath condensed as soon as it left her nostrils! It *was* cold out here.

Oh! That reminded her of childhood winters with heavy snow, and the wonderful warm fires on Grannie's farm. Then there had been nothing better than snuggling up to Grannie on the sofa in front of the fire, when they came inside from their chores. They shared the home made woolly blanket, and cradled a mug of hot chocolate. It was absolute bliss, and then Grannie would tell stories.

This was also where she had learned how to read. First by recognising the odd letter then word until one day she could read along and spot when Grannie left a word out on purpose-teasing her. The special memories made her smile.

Seagulls that were flying around the ferry were doing amazing aerobatics, their white plumage contrasted beautifully against the icy-blue winter sky. They were screeching, diving and fighting over whatever the propeller churned up in the wash behind the ferry. The steady drone of the engine accompanied their mocking calls, whenever they successfully managed to steal someone else's food.

The strong engine deep down in the bowels of the ferry made vibrations that could be felt through the soles of her walking boots. Her warm hands in the gloves were holding on to the sturdy railings, which she had to tiptoe to look over. From here she could see the brilliant white bow wave against the deep green water. The railings made her feel safe, unlike the island, with its little white crofts up there on the green hillsides, which did not feel safe at all!

Yet it had drawn her to it like a strong magnet. She scanned the island with her hand to her brow trying to work out which one was 'Harbour View'? Surely with a name like that she should be able to see it from here, as she could now see the large jetty. 'Harbour' was perhaps a bit of an exaggeration. This was all so new! And it had all happened so quickly.

# 2

It was just another one of the, already far too many, awful days. It was the beginning of December and Christmas preparations were well underway. As well as working full time she was busy baking and filling the freezer with sausage rolls, mince pies and stuffings. The home made presents had been under way for months, and were almost finished. It was hectic at times when there was only one to do it all, but she loved it.

It was a cold, dark morning and it was raining sleet. Her boots got soaked waiting for the bus. Cars driving too close to the curb sent sprays of water over the pavement. The tube was packed with commuters like sardines in a tin, and people coughed and sneezed, spreading winter bugs. Their wet clothes steamed up the windows, and to top it, the train had to stop in a claustrophobic tunnel between two stations, as there was 'an incident' on the line. They all knew what that meant, but even an awful thing like a suicide couldn't make these strangers talk to each other. Only deep sighs and heaven sent eyes and glances at wristwatches indicated the passenger's irritation of the delay. Where *had* compassion gone?

When she finally did arrive at work her boss had looked disapprovingly at the clock shaking his head and he had been absolutely impossible. All morning he was nagging and short tempered, sighing and barking orders from his office across the room, and by the afternoon tea break Vera had simply had enough. To get out before she said something terrible, that would only get her fired on the spot, she made an excuse saying that she had a terrible headache.

The tube home was equally packed and she felt that she was being squeezed from all sides both mentally and physically.

The whole situation was simply unbearable, but she had to go to work to make ends meet, so what could she do? She'd had to give up her beloved nursing when she looked after Martin, during his long illness. As she had nursed him at home until he died, and often alone, her slipped disc from years of nursing finally finished her beloved career. The desk job in the hospital was all they could offer her; not at all ideal, but it was a job and meant that she kept her pension. The only silver lining was that it was a nine to five job, with no nights, evenings or weekends. A real bonus in fact, but she did miss caring for the patients.

When she got home, she ran herself a hot bath. That soothed the tense muscles and helped her to relax. In the evening she went to her monthly beekeeping meeting. The beekeepers were a jolly bunch and she always enjoyed their company.

It just so happened that someone had received a letter from the Scottish division. The island of Strathsay needed a new beekeeper. The last beekeeper had died in the autumn of last year, after a few months of ill health. He had not been able to winter the bees in the late summer and consequently they perished during the very cold winter.

That was it! This was her get out ticket! Her beekeeping friends encouraged her; they could all see what a fantastic opportunity this was for her. They had seen her wither after Martin's long illness and his death four years ago. With her many years of experience, she would be ideal for the job.

She left the meeting early to go home to ring the children. She was all fired up, and very excited. Michael who was a carpenter and boat builder, was living in Colchester with his girlfriend Helen who was a school-teacher and Ruth was a vet student in Cambridge in her penultimate year. As soon as she got home, she made a pot of tea and rang them, even though it was past nine o'clock; the normal cut off time for polite phone calls, and she was thrilled that they both thought that it was a great idea and gave her their blessings. They too could see that this was a wonderful opportunity for her.

Then she rang to Lisa, her best friend since their days together as student nurses many decades ago, to tell her of her plans.

"You can't do that!" The words flew straight out of Lisa's mouth. She always spoke her mind, which was one of Lisa's many qualities that Vera really appreciated.

"Why not?" It didn't take very much for Vera to begin to doubt whether she had actually bitten off too much. Her wobbly self-confidence was easily destroyed.

"But I thought it would be really exciting. Wouldn't it?"

"Yes it would, but you'll be far away! Very very far away! And I'm going to miss you dreadfully." She didn't mince her words. "What'll I do without you?" she sniffed and Vera could hear that Lisa was becoming emotional.

"Yes but Lisa, I am so fed up with my boss, I really can't stand him or the work. And now this amazing opportunity has come like a present sent from heaven - actually I wonder if Martin has got a finger in it too? He knew of my dream to live in a croft – I've told you about that before. Remember?"

"Yes, I do vaguely remember a conversation about that. But it was years ago, and I didn't think that you would make it happen. One thing is dreaming about something and another is pulling up the tent pegs and actually move away."

"Well Lisa I really want you to try to see the prospect from my point of view."

"But I can't do that Vera. All I can see is that I am going to miss you dreadfully."

Vera was now ready to drop the whole idea. Her lack of self-confidence was in full bloom and Lisa had well and truly squashed all the previous enthusiasm.

Lisa noticed that Vera was getting upset as she became quiet at the other end, and being the really good friend that she was, she said.

"Hey! - I know it's late, but why don't I pop over? We'll light the fire and have a cup of tea and then we can talk it through face to face."

"Orrh I don't know Lisa - I'm not much company now. I need to think about all this. - I was so happy when I came home, now I'm all confused and tired, I think I'll just go to bed."

"Right! I am hopping in the car straight away. Light the fire and put the kettle on. I am on my way!" Lisa didn't wait for a reply, and quickly explained the situation to her husband Bert. She told him it could be late and that she might even stay the night at Vera's. He was used to Lisa's sudden improvisations, and wasn't surprised at all that she felt that she had to go over to Vera.

In the car Lisa had time to mull over the situation and by the time she arrived, she had changed her tune. Of course Vera must take this opportunity. Lisa had seen with her own eyes how the bullying boss had undermined Vera's self confidence, and she knew that Vera deserved so much better. It was good to see that her spirit hadn't been completely extinguished, and she decided that she was going to give Vera all the support she needed. So she stopped on the way to buy a bottle of fizz and a bouquet of flowers. She knew that she wouldn't be able to drive home, but it would not be the first time that she had stayed over for that exact same reason.

It was a tired, red-eyed Vera that opened the door, hugging the woolly cardigan which hung from her drooping shoulders. She was indeed a sorry sight and Lisa cringed and felt guilty. It was such a surprise for Vera to see Lisa standing there with a bottle, a bunch of flowers and a big smile.

"What's all this now?" She mopped her nose and welcomed Lisa with a hug.

"Yes! I've had a think, and I've changed my mind! We are going to celebrate that you have the gumption to think that this is a good idea. It's not just a good idea Vera! It's a brilliant idea, so go and get the glasses, we are going to talk about adventure now!"

They laughed and went into the sitting room, where a cheery fire was already burning brightly.
Lisa listened carefully to the information Vera had, and the more she heard the better the whole thing sounded.

"Have you spoken to the children? And what did they think?"

"They both said 'go for it mum!' That's why I got so upset when I told you and you said, 'don't do it.' I was so excited that I rang you straight away, so your reaction was a real let down to be honest."

"Well! I am right behind the plans now. So pour us some of that lovely bubbly, will you!"

They googled the island and much to their surprise there was even a croft for sale!
It was called Harbour View, and had been for sale since the summer. It was completely newly
renovated, with a new roof, double glazed windows, and much to their surprise even a brand new bathroom. It looked absolutely lovely, and Vera fell in love with it instantly. It was late before they finally got to bed, and by then they had giggled, cried and laughed and spoken about all the aspects of the move. They made a pro's and con's list, and pro's had won big time.

Once she had made the decision to take up this new challenge, everything became so easy and just fell into place. Just like stepping stones, one was put in front of her, and the next and the next.

This was a rare opportunity and she was not going to let it pass her by! She put in an offer on the croft, which was immediately accepted. Then she put her house on the market and sold it within days to a really nice young couple, who was expecting a baby in May. And...this was the best feeling ever!

When she finally walked into the boss's office with her resignation letter in her hand and said:

"I am moving to Scotland and as I'm owed so much holiday, I shall clear my desk this morning and leave at lunchtime."

Just like that! Then she dropped the envelope in front of him. His turkey neck and double chin wobbled and the jaw dropped. "Uhmm, b-b-b-but," was all he could say, shaking his head in total disbelief. Small pearls of sweat appeared on his greasy bald scalp and speechless he just stared at her, reaching for the mug of coffee with his cigarette stained fingers. Then she turned on her heel and walked slowly out of the office feeling at least a meter taller. With her back to him she smiled from ear to ear and whispered "YESSS!" As she closed his door behind her she leant on it briefly. What a relief!

She walked back to her desk and felt how her shoulders slowly sank and found their normal resting place as the muscles at last could relax and lengthen. She didn't even know that she had been so tense.

She sat down relieved and elated, and texted Lisa,
"*I did it!*"

Her reply arrived instantaneously, *"Whoop-whoop let's celebrate! Meet me at Ricardo's*
*at 18.30, I'll book a table".*

Then she went to make a cup of tea. She was miles away on the island, mentally she had already moved in.

To the extent that she wondered about silly things like what sort of plants would thrive on the deep window sills. Maybe they could even be used like a little mini greenhouse to bring on plants indoors in the spring. And she wondered how cold it would get in the winter; maybe she would even get ice flowers on the inside of the windows. She could see the pretty patterns in her mind's eye, remembering the cold frosty mornings on Grannie's farm. She cradled the mug, dreaming away, but realised after a little while that there were actually things to see to, if she really was going to leave at lunchtime.

# 3

And here she was on the ferry, and the dream was finally a reality. She watched as the captain expertly navigated the buoyed channel. There were rocks that only just broke the surface of the deep green water. White frothy water washed over the submerged granite, that it was so important for him to avoid.

As they got closer she could see a small white lighthouse at the end of the pier, it was blinking red. And then she noticed several people already waiting on the pier, which had been built from huge granite boulders. The top had been covered in concrete to make it sturdy and flat. The pier curved gently and provided a safe sheltered area, protected from the worst weather.

*'Solid and strong just like my little croft, which will keep me safe and protect me from whatever life has in store to throw at me now.'*

She looked at the green gently sloping hills and somehow the island seemed familiar.

"I'm sure I'll be very happy here!" Oops! She realised that she'd actually spoken out loud. A little embarrassed she looked around to see if anybody had heard her. Luckily she was still the only one outside on deck. Everyone else was sitting comfortably inside in the warmth, chatting or reading and enjoying a warm drink. It was a very comfortable ferry, which she could certainly recommend to her coming visitors. Of which she was sure there would be many.

Big letters on the building at the end of the pier said Strathsay Post Office. And she spotted an old-fashioned red telephone box too. Behind the post office was a long row of terraced cottages with many chimneys. They were all smoking, so they were obviously occupied, and not just holiday homes. The smoke just rose gently as if from smouldering fires; it looked very cosy and somehow felt welcoming.

The old granite church with its square solid tower stood proud, strong and protective above the village. The sun was shining on the huge stained glass windows. *'I shall look forward to seeing them from the inside'*.

A land rover with a trailer had been parked on the pier, *'I wonder how they managed to reverse that out there, it can't have been easy'.* The difficulty in reversing backwards into tight parking spaces had never been something she enjoyed. The people waiting on the pier were all dressed in big, patterned pullovers and were busy talking to each other and she could see how they were gesticulating.

Then as they got even closer she noticed that there were several boxes stacked up on the pier, presumably ready to be sent back with the ferry as it returned to the mainland. *'I wonder what the islanders are making and even selling.'* What did she have, she wondered, that she could bring to the island community apart from the obvious bee keeping skills?

*'Well we'll see, I am sure I shall be useful somehow. I am quite sure I have 'been sent' to this island for a reason, and I am very keen to find out what the learning experiences are going to be for me here.'*

To start with she was going to write some articles about her experiences of moving to and living in a small community on an island. She had been in contact with a magazine editor who had been very interested to hear about her brave life change. 'Write little and often' had been the editor's advice, and in return Vera would be paid for her contributions. She wouldn't exactly be short of money as the house had sold for much more than the croft had cost her, and in addition she had Martin's generous pension, and now also her own. She had forgotten about that. But it was good to have something to get her teeth into, until she could start the bee keeping in earnest.

She would of course also keep the bee keepers informed of her various findings with regards to bee-keeping, they were after all the ones that had encouraged her to move here. She would be starting from scratch. Hoping to get some of the islanders interested too.

The young deckhand, Callum, who had also functioned as the ticket collector, and provider of hot drinks, sandwiches and snacks on the journey from the mainland, came out to get the mooring warps ready. The skipper slowed the engine down, and skilfully guided the ferry on to the quay. It had several old car tyres tied on to wooden planks protecting the wood from the ferry's tough steel hull. In return the contraption also protected the hull from the huge granite boulders, which on a rough day would, no doubt, do a lot of damage to anything that got near them.

Vera found it all fascinating; she had never witnessed a ship being moored as closely as this. She could hear the skipper's instructions to Callum on his walkie-talkie, and his responses, which were mostly "aye-aye". Sometimes he just turned and looked up at the skipper and gave him a 'thumbs up'. This was obviously very careful teamwork.

The person on the pier who was receiving the warps looked around and shouted, "Stand clear!" just before they were thrown ashore. He quickly fastened the bow-line and then ran along the quay to receive the line from the stern. Once the boat was safely moored, the captain slowed the engine right down to idling and first then could Callum fit the gangway, and the passengers were allowed to disembark.

They all had bags, boxes and crates of various shapes and sizes.

But Vera had the largest suitcases of all the passengers and several boxes, which Callum very kindly carried ashore, and stacked neatly.

She searched the quay for Mr Morrison who was her contact person on the island. They'd had several conversations already on the telephone. He'd said that he would be wearing a big blue sweater, and a red woolly hat, and if it was raining oilskins "that used to be yellow!" he had laughed. She couldn't actually see anyone wearing an outfit like he had described at the moment.

She then remembered that he'd said, "If I am not on the quay, you will probably find me in the post office as it gets pretty cold waiting on the quay this time of year."
There were hearty greetings of "Helloooo!" in the lovely Scottish accent and big warm hugs, for some of the passengers.

*'Wouldn't it just have been so nice if there had been someone here to welcome me too!'* She thought with a sad little twinge. She took a deep breath and thought to herself, *'Well now! Chin up! You're a big girl and this is a new adventure, so: Here goes!'* She slung on the rucksack and stepped on to the gangway and went ashore. She had arrived on Strathsay.

# 4

The passengers from the ferry began to drift away in small groups to all sorts of waiting transportation. Someone had a big old-fashioned wooden cart. What a clatter the metal-clad huge wheels made. Another person had brought a pram, there was no child in sight, so there was plenty of room for bags and belongings. A man had brought his wheelbarrow; he had received a crate of chickens. *'Mmmm fresh eggs!'* she smiled; she had toyed with the idea of keeping a few chickens herself up here.

All her belongings had been left on the quay and Callum assured her that they would be completely safe. She looked at the bags and remembered that she would need some matches and milk. She began to walk towards the post office shop. She also wanted to go in and say hello and introduce herself.

Mr Morrison had telephoned weeks ago to say that her order from John Lewis had arrived. He asked if it was ok to deliver it all to the cottage with the driver. She had told him that it was a dining table and chairs, a sofa, a bed, mattress and bedside tables. He had asked if she needed help putting it all up, and as she did, he said that he would be very happy to do so for her. Did she want him to get it ready before she arrived? An offer she had gratefully accepted. She was so excited to see all the new things when she finally got there.

As she walked in through the post office door with the colourful sign saying: " WELCOME TO THE HUB" a little bell that was attached to the door tinkled, and a homely smell of fresh coffee greeted her.

There were lots of groceries for sale, including some very tempting vegetables and fresh fruit.
"Come in! Come in! And welcome!" A smiling lady with an unruly mob of red curly hair, dressed in jeans and a big colourful Fair Isle sweater, came towards her and took Vera's hand and looked straight into her eyes,

"I'm Mrs Morrison, but everybody calls me Mrs M. You must be Vera! Welcome! Do sit yerself deyn, have a coffee and a wee drram, it's sooo cooold eyt therre!"

"Everybody!" She turned to the others in the room." This is Vera! The new lady in Harbour View!"   She opened her arm toward Vera in an introductory way. Vera nodded and smiled and they all smiled back and lifted their dram glasses or mugs to welcome her.

They were sitting at little tables; which had red and white gingham tablecloths and a tea light in a glass candle holder and some even had small flowers in a little vase.

Vera happily accepted the kind invite. She took off the big coat and her woolly hat and shook out the imprisoned curls; it was warm and welcoming in here.

She hadn't realised how exhausted she actually was, until she sat down in the warm room. It had been a long journey, on top of very busy weeks of preparing, packing and storing her belongings. And now she had all the unpacking to look forward to as well.

The goodbye party at Lisa's the evening before last, had gone on far too long. She had wanted an early night, but there were simply too many to say goodbye to, and she had gone to bed much too late. Lisa and Bert had brought her to the station in the morning all ready with a packed lunch and a flask of tea. Tears had inevitably flowed. This was big, not just for Vera but for all of them.

After several changes she'd arrived at the Harbour Hotel in the evening, just in time for dinner and ready for the ferry to the island early the following morning. It had been a long journey both mentally and physically.

The people around her were chatting and laughing, it seemed like it was a very lively place and not for nothing called 'THE HUB'. Their accent was strong and it was impossible to understand what they were saying when they talked amongst themselves, but they sounded jolly and there were lots of warm smiles to Vera. But it did feel a bit lonely, 'If only Martin had been here' she caught herself thinking, and felt her eyes welling up. Mrs M noticed it straight away and said,

"Yes! This is what the cold does to your eyes, makes them water, right?!"

Vera was grateful for the kind rescuing remark. And... this was where she found Mr Morrison; it turned out that the land rover on the quay was his, and he had then been waiting for her in the post office, as he had many jobs.

He was the island's general handyman, and he served coffee just now in The Hub. He delivered post, parcels, and groceries and helped out with any problems?...He was the island's 'man who can', she learnt from the others.

He brought her coffee tray over and said,

"Hellooo! Vera", with a beaming smile.

Vera stood up to greet him, but was only reaching to his broad chest and looked up into his twinkling blue eyes. He was a real Viking with his wavy blond hair and bushy red beard. The huge blue pullover emphasised his enormous shoulders. He blocked out the view of the rest of the room. He introduced himself with a warm smile and strong handshake. Her little hand completely disappeared in his.

"Welcome! I trust you have had a good journey. The weather has certainly been kind to you."

*'What a gentle giant,'* she smiled back. He looked just like she had imagined, just a lot bigger.

She noticed the little jug of water on the tray and Mr Morrison could see that she was puzzled.

"Whisky is always served with a jug of water in Scotland. The water helps to enhance the taste, every one mixes to their own taste." That was something new to Vera. The coffee was most welcome and the wee dram warmed her physically and the piece of homemade shortbread boosted her energy.

He told her that there were three other crofts and a farm quite nearby on the track that went all the way out to the lighthouse, which meant that the post van would be passing at least once a day. All she would have to do if she wanted him to stop was to hang a red rag in the canopy over the front door so it could be seen from the road.

"Easy! " He laughed, "or you can also just ring, but the other signal might get me there faster if I am already out on my rounds and you find that you need me. Sometimes we have problems with the phone line so then we have to use other means of communication. Do you have a torch? We do have power cuts at times too."

He also told her that he would be very happy to bring groceries if she phoned and left a list. Food could also be dropped off by one of the supermarkets on the mainland. It would then arrive on the ferry, and then be brought directly to her door by him. What a service! Vera nodded, impressed. But he hastily added,

"We don't use that so much, as we cater for everything here at the post office and you only have to ask and we'll get it for ye!" He smiled and winked with a sideways nod towards Mrs Morrison, who was now behind the glass counter of the post-office at the other end of the room. She was wearing her white postmistress's cap, with its black lacquered peak, gold braid and sparkling emblem, placed on top of her beautiful unruly red curls.

They had 3 children, two were still on the island but the eldest had gone to the senior school on the mainland and only returned home at the weekend. Vera almost felt as if she knew the family already.

"You just sit and wait here, and I'll call for you when I'm ready." Mr Morrison ventured back out in the chilly breeze. He went to the quay and Callum helped load all her belongings onto the trailer. She stayed in the warm HUB and chatted with Mrs M. who was an energetic and very helpful lady, with rosy apple cheeks. A sure sign of someone who liked to be outside. Vera wondered whether she actually managed to get any time outdoors with her busy life, being mother, wife, shopkeeper and postmistress.

She told Vera that people tended to meet on Friday evening at the Village Hall, for a chat, some food and a dram. Sometimes there would be a dance or a game of some sort. Sometimes a speaker would be invited or they would be showing a film. Vera would always be most welcome, and she said that it wouldn't take much more than a good twenty minutes to walk from the croft down to the village hall situated just behind the post office.

"It is really quite straightforward, but it is a good idea to walk with either a stick or a pole, on the unmade road. You will be surprised how much you can see in the dark, once your eyes adjust, as there are no street lights here to blind your night vision." She added reassuringly.

Vera was intrigued. Where she had come from the streetlights would be on from dusk to dawn. Night vision! Not a word she had heard for many a year.

Mrs M continued, "There is a notice about tomorrow over there," she pointed at a noticeboard. Vera went over to have a look at it. It announced a ceilidh, with a fish pie supper and ginger-cake with ice-cream for dessert, all for £5. There were many messages about things for sale, hands needed for this and that. This was obviously an important communication place for the islanders.

"What is a ceilidh?" This was a new word for Vera

"Scottish country dancing, and great fun. There will be a live orchestra and a caller who tells us what to do. Do come along, it really is a good evening!"

Then Mr Morrison pulled up outside with the trailer and beeped. Vera picked up her things, said goodbye and jumped into the car, and together they began the last little bit of the journey up towards the croft that was going to be her new home from now on. Mr Morrison pointed ahead to the one that was Harbour View explaining who lived in the other crofts on the hill side.

"Oh! I can't wait!" She smiled, and clapped her hands in front of her mouth and tapped her feet excitedly on the floor of the car.

The closer they got the more inviting it looked. There was thin smoke coming from both chimneys. The house looked really well cared for; the grass outside was neatly edged. The fence was painted white.

Mr Morrison remembered that he had an envelope in his pocket. "To Vera" it said on it. Inside was a key to the front door and a welcome note with all the information she needed. Little things like where the stopcock could be found, where the electricity meter was situated, and that on a nail in the kitchen was the key to the back door and the wood shed, which incidentally was full of wood and peat, seasoned and ready to use.

"We normally don't lock our doors here, but I thought I'd better as I thought it would maybe worry you if I hadn't. I've also turned on the AGA and you are really lucky! It's one of these modern electric ones."

Vera smiled at him; she had never used an AGA before, but did know of people who wouldn't live without theirs. She was very pleased that she had left her home in a clean and tidy way, completely ready to move into.

She had made it as easy as possible for the delightful young couple, who had been so enthusiastic about the house when they came to look around. She had arranged for some flowers to be delivered to them tomorrow Friday, when they would be moving in, just to say 'Welcome to your new home'.

Mr Morrison slowed down and stopped the car. Vera was out of the door before he had even turned the engine off.

# 5

The wooden front door was indeed very old. The soft wood between the year rings had been worn away by wind, salt, sand and rain. This gave the wood a rippled effect. And it *did* have a little glass-canopy with the ornate brackets! How strange. It also had an old metal door knocker shaped as an anchor-and somehow that seemed familiar too. She tapped it, tap-taptap! Just to warn the house that she was now coming! What a lovely solid sound it made.

She took the key out of the envelope; it was large, ornate and very old-fashioned. It was obviously made with great skill and was beautifully decorated with Celtic patterns. When she inserted it into the keyhole it turned smoothly and easily with a little click. She pressed the latch down and the heavy old door swung gently into the hallway with a long disapproving squeak from the hinges.

"Oh yes, I completely forgot that! It needs a squirt of WD40, I'll bring it next time I come by." Said Mr Morrison right behind her.

The wooden staircase going upstairs on the left of the little hall-way, was bathed in the light that poured down from the very bright room above. The door immediately to the left led into the kitchen/ dining room/ lounge, which was another wonderfully light room despite the low ceiling, as it had several windows.

"I love it!" She exclaimed, still standing on the big granite doorstep and turned and looked at Mr Morrison behind her.

"I absolutely love it!" and without thinking about it she flung her arms round him and hugged him.

"Oh sorry, I got a bit carried away there," she quickly apologised, but he just smiled and said,

"I would've hugged you back but I've got these! " and nodded with an apologetic smile down towards the bags in his hands. That made them both laugh.

"Let's go in!" He said.

As she entered, she immediately had deja vu, strangely it all felt familiar. She reckoned that it was because she had spent such a long time imagining living in a croft. It was a real coming-home feeling and she found it very reassuring. She had never experienced anything like this before. It felt wonderfully peaceful.

It pleased her that the rooms were so light; from the window on the left in the sitting room she could see all the way down to the post office and the quay. It was a perfect place for the dining table. There was another window on the other side of the wood-burning stove. The last window was above the kitchen sink, and the full length of the worktop. It looked out over the garden and towards the hills. There was a little back porch with a back door leading out to a little enclosure. A nice corner with the woodshed on the right and made a patio that was sheltered from the wind. It even had a large glass veranda roof.

*'I'll be able to sit out there on summer evenings with candles, and not be bothered by the dew falling. Being so far north, the summer evenings will be long and light.'* She was dreaming away, when she heard Mr Morrison say,

"Where would you like this box?"

"Please just put everything in the hall, then I'll sort it later. Thank you!"

She went out of the back door and checked out the outbuilding, which had two doors. One was to a sort of garden shed, and the other was the wood store, and it *was* true there was plenty of seasoned wood and peat.

On the large chopping block lay a tiny key, which had a very thin plaited light blue woollen loop on it- *'what a beautiful piece of work, and what a strange place for it to be;-it's almost as if it's been put there on purpose for me to find it, I'll bring it inside to keep it safe.'*

She was sure it must be of importance and felt lucky that she had spotted it as it could so easily have fallen down between the logs. As she picked it up, she noticed that it felt warm, *'how odd'* she thought, and went back into the cottage.

"Look what I just found in the wood shed!" She lifted it so Mr Morrison could see it, "isn't it beautiful?"

"It certainly is." he agreed.

She hung it on the wall in the kitchen where there was a spare nail, and went on exploring. In the hall there were two more doors. The door straight across the hallway lead into the bedroom. Here there was another wood burner, but in this room it was smaller and situated on the northern wall. There were two windows facing east and west and there were also plenty of built-in cupboards on the wall behind the door to the hall, backing on to the bathroom wall. The bed faced the window looking out over the sea. *'What a view to wake up to! Martin would have loved this!'*

The door straight ahead to the right of the stairs in the hall; went into the bathroom, which was both spacious, modern and really sparkling. She absolutely loved all the immaculate white porcelain. In particular she liked the wall hung toilet and the lovely streamlined sink, with its gleaming mixer tap, not to mention the bath tub…*'oh I can just imagine a lovely relaxing bath with candles, lavender oil and classical music in the background, mmm…'* Then she noticed that the water in the toilet bowl was amber-coloured. She thought that Mr Morrison might have forgotten to flush it and quickly pressed the button, but the new water was just as golden. She pointed this out to Mr Morrison,

"Well that's just the peat Vera! All the water on the island is this colour,"

"Peat?" she repeated, surprised. "Well that will take a little getting used to. I wonder what it tastes like? I'm not sure if I fancy brushing my teeth in that, and I wonder what will the tea taste like?"

"I suppose we could give it a try by making some!" He hinted with a wink.

"Yes that is a brilliant idea, let's find the kettle, it will be in the box marked with the red crosses."

That box had all the essentials for the first day; kettle, teapot, tea and coffee, mugs, kitchen roll, and toilet paper, washing up liquid, tea towel, food, not anything fancy, but essentials like long life milk, homemade flapjacks and a tin of soup and baked beans.

"You don't really need a kettle, you have the AGA; look there is a kettle for it over there. The AGA will boil it faster than the electric kettle."

He was right, the kettle was soon singing, and she poured the boiling water into the teapot, and left it to brew and then went to explore upstairs. She came up the stairs to a surprisingly spacious big room the whole length of the house. It had a wooden floor and white sloping walls with 6 Velux windows in the roof, which made it delightfully light. There were storage cupboards under the eaves.

From the eastern side she could see the sea and all the way to the mainland in the far distance and from the others the hills, '*and I will be able to look at the stars on clear nights, oh what a brilliant room for painting!*' She was so excited. There were some big ornate cast iron grills on the floor at either end of the room. Looking down through them she could look into the kitchen and the bedroom, the grills allowed the warm air from the wood burners below to rise and heat the upstairs. She concluded that the roof must be incredibly well insulated, if that was all it took to keep it warm, and it would be an excellent guest bedroom. She was quite sure she would be inundated with visitors, so this room was a real godsend.

The next essential box was marked with blue and had bedding and towels, pillows, duvet, toilet bag, nightclothes and a clean set of clothes, and most importantly candles and a torch. She was immensely glad she had remembered to buy the matches at the post office. How could she have forgotten to pack something so important? Anyway she had them now and that was the main thing.

It didn't take them long to empty the trailer and the lounge and hall area was now chocker block with boxes and belongings. Next to the wood-burner stood a fantastic contraption, it was a large willow basket on two wheels with a long handle, which made it very easy to manoeuvre out to the woodshed for filling up, and it was already full of wood! There were small kindling sticks that would catch fire quickly and some bigger pieces of wood and also some peat. Mr Morrison saw to the fires whilst Vera made a cup of tea for them both. He explained that the peat would burn slowly through the night and keep the croft warm. It didn't take long before there was a lovely glow in both stoves giving off lots of heat. He turned the air inlets right down, and they sat down with their big mugs of tea and some of Vera's homemade flapjacks.

"Umm these are good!" He said, munching away. He told Vera that the post office shop was very happy to buy all sorts of home made produce, jam, marmalade, pickles, cakes and home grown vegetables, "and these flapjacks will be very popular, I'm sure of that." He said taking another bite.

Vera nodded approvingly at the tea; it really tasted very good indeed.

"The flapjacks are made with honey, that's what makes them so good."

It felt good in the cottage, it was untidy and messy just now, but it was warm and already felt like home. She thanked Mr Morrison for his kind help, and asked what his charge would be for all the work he had done. He declined, most severely, it was almost as if she had offended him by offering to pay him for his kindness.

"Of course I would help you move in," he smiled, and rested his big hands on her shoulders. "We want you to be happy here Vera. We all try to be helpful, that is just how we are. You will be happy here. I know it!"

Vera's eyes welled up, but he didn't see that, as he had already turned to leave, and went down to the car with his arm in the air to goodbye.

She had felt like hugging him again, it had been a very long time since she had felt so warmly welcomed and was a bit overcome by it all. She mopped a tear with her hanky.

Off he went; back down the hill with the trailer. What an extremely kind and helpful man, Vera was so impressed.

He was the complete and utter opposite to her boss, who had been the main reason that she had decided so quickly to accept the move to the island, when the opportunity so suddenly had presented itself, such a surprisingly short time ago.

She needed a new beginning and peace of mind to recover from the long time of being slowly ground down by her awful boss. She had lost a lot of her self-confidence. Accepting both verbal and emotional abuse from him and now, having escaped, she couldn't really believe that she had put up with it all. Why on earth had she put up with him for so long?

It had been anything to keep the peace, the job and the income. But not any more!

Her spirit had not been completely destroyed. She was recognising little snippets of her good old self that were beginning to wake up again. Given time she would recover. She knew that, and this was the perfect place. Surrounded by people who had a positive attitude, and a kind and helpful way of life.

Her own motto had always been 'be to others as you would like them to be to you', and that would certainly work in this place. She stood in the door and watched him disappear down the hill, waving and beeping to various houses and people he passed. She held onto the warm mug, cradling it with two hands holding it close to her chest. It felt lonely without his company. She looked round the hall and lounge. Where to begin? There was so much to be done. Behind the door on a hook she noticed a red rag-the one Mr Morrison had told her to hang on the canopy if she needed him to call in.

# 6

The sun was sparkling on the water. It was heading for the horizon and the shadows were already growing long. The days were obviously much shorter up here this time of the year. The sun was now pouring into the kitchen window. What a marvellous bright living space with sun all day long.

It wouldn't be long before there would be much more strength and warmth in the rays. Then she could have the doors open, but for now it was time to get organised for the evening and night. Before it got completely dark it would be a good idea to find the fuse box, and the torch and the candles. The matches had already found their place on the shelf near the wood burner.

The wood basket was full enough for the night and as the AGA was on she would be able to cook a meal. She went round the house and tested all the light bulbs. She checked the doors and the windows, and went into the bedroom, which was pleasantly warm. She found the bedding in the boxes, and whilst she made the bed she opened the windows to air the room. Having the wood burner in there, Mr Morrison had advised her that she would actually have to keep the window slightly open, otherwise she would wake up with a nasty headache in the morning.

She could hear the sea through the open windows. The waves washed gently on to the shore and the seagulls were still calling to one another. She also recognised a curlew's calls.

She could watch the sea out of the eastern window from her bed, *'It will be nice to sit here in the morning and watch the sun rise, whilst I drink my morning tea.'* Tea in bed had always been so enjoyable but reserved for weekends only- But not anymore!

The mobile phone rang; it was Ruth. She wanted to hear how the day had gone. Vera was glad that there was still tea in the pot, as she knew that this would be a rather long conversation.

Whilst they talked, a pink tinted dusk settled gently over the island. She lit the little tea lights in the glass candleholders as they talked. They sparkled and spread a lovely glow in the room. Ruth was excited to hear of the loft room and the wood burners, never mind the AGA. She would definitely come and visit very soon, as she couldn't wait to see the new place.

As they talked Vera noticed that the wind began to gather strength. She could hear it in the chimney and turned the air inlets right down on the wood burner. She asked if Ruth by any chance had seen or heard the weather forecast, which she hadn't. So when they had finished talking Vera went for a quick tour round the outside of the house to make sure there was nothing that could fly around in the wind. Maybe it was because of the coming wind that the gulls had been screeching? She would make a note of her observations; there would be so much to both learn and write about.

Coming back inside she was so pleased to find it cosy and safe indoors, and made a mental note of the time, 18.05, oh bother then she was too late for the weather forecast on the radio. It was only a little portable transistor radio, but it was enough for her needs. She would go and find it straight away.

The list of boxes was invaluable; she'd had enough foresight to write on every box what was in it, and made a list of every box's contents, so it was very easy to find box no 7, which was the one with the radio. Here she also found a tablecloth, and more candles, which she put on the dining table. Plates and cutlery were put on the table, as she found the things and put them in the cupboards, the cutlery she put in the drawer to the left of the sink, right under the practical draining board.

The fridge, which stood in the back porch, had a little freezer compartment. There would be room for slices of lime and lemons, ready to be put straight into fizzy water or even in a gin and tonic. Above it was a coat rail, how smart! That would keep coats warm and dry.

She was making a mental list as she worked around the kitchen of things she would need. She placed a piece of paper and a pen next to her plate, so she could write the shopping list as she had her meal. She would definitely have to go shopping tomorrow; it would have to be a rather big one this first shop. She was glad that Mr Morrison had offered, 'you shop, I'll drop' he had said laughing copying Tesco's logo.

The phone rang, it was the landline, 'brrrring-briiiing' it went, what a nice ring it had. "Weeell gyd eve'nin!" It was Mr Morrison's well known voice, "I'm just ringing to make shyrr all's wheale and ye're not blo-in aweh up theeeerrr." How very kind of him to enquire to her, she thanked him and reassured him that all was well and thanked him again for all his help today and said she would be coming down to the post office tomorrow to shop.

"Weeeell ye have a pleasant night thehn" he said and rang off.

She poured herself another cup of tea, and served her meal, and sat down to eat. She had tuned the transistor to smooth classics at seven on Classic Fm. It was lovely to hear the wind in the chimney and the crackle in the wood burner accompanying Smetana's The Moldau. This was her absolute favourite piece of music and she took this as a good omen; that it was played on her very first evening in her new home. She felt surprisingly at home already, relaxed, at ease, happy and very very tired. She went to find Martin's picture, he had to be here too, and placed it on the mantelpiece.

She undid her serviette from its ring. This little silver ring, which she had been given at the occasion of her first communion had been part of her daily life ever since. It was shaped almost like two hands meeting saying thank you for the meal in store. She sent a quiet but very appreciative thank you "upwards" before tucking in to the well-deserved meal.

She decided to leave the shopping list until breakfast, cleared up in the kitchen, and made her goodnight cup of tea. Then she turned the wood burner's air-inlet right down low after putting the peat on the embers, just as Mr Morrison had shown her to do for the night.

She turned out the lights and then blew out the candles. This was a routine she had learned from Grannie, "always turn the lights off first, then you won't leave a burning candle by mistake", she had said time and time again. Good old fashioned advice that had stuck in Vera's mind. Then she went to the bathroom, which by now was warm too.

The AGA heated the hot water and the under-floor heating pipes. What a luxury! *'How lovely it will be to get into a warm bathroom in the morning.'*

This was something she hadn't been used to in the old house, as the heating was always off at night. She had always been the first one up, and in recent years the only one up, and she had never had the luxury of the bathroom being warm and inviting in the morning. But not anymore.

Snuggled into the new bed, she turned out the light on the bedside table. She would just sit in the dark and look out, whilst drinking the tea. With the lights on the window was just a black hole in the wall. With the light off she could see little glowing lights here and there from the other crofts across the bay. But what was that on the windowsill? She turned the light back on, and got up. It was the little key from the woodshed, but how on earth had it got in here? She left it there and went back to bed. Intrigued.

The buoys on the water were blinking red and green, in the channel that guided the ships safely into the harbour. The beam from the lighthouse swept over the water.

When the tea was drunk, she snuggled down warm and happy. She turned on to her side, made a deep contented sigh, and fell asleep straight away to the sound of the wind in the chimney, whilst making mental plans for tomorrow.

# 7

As she slowly surfaced the next morning, she knew that the room was bright, without even opening her eyes; and then she noticed the quietness. All she could hear was birds chirping and the gentle swish of the waves. It actually sounded like the sea breathed. She opened her eyes and recognised the bedroom, and remembered how she had looked out at the blinking buoys and the water and how wonderful it had been. She pushed herself up in the bed. Now she could see the hills of the mainland across the sound of Strathsay.

*'Oh yes! This is of course my new home'*, she smiled to herself and stretched.

In London the morning sky, if she could see it for clouds, had always been crisscrossed by vapour trails from aeroplanes. And there was a constant drone of traffic. Here all she could see was the sky and the water and not a cloud in sight. Both were being painted slightly pink on the horizon as dawn was gently announcing its arrival. She looked at her watch 6.15. She couldn't remember ever waking up by herself at this time. Apart from the first many months of her bereavement, when she used to wake early to be met again and again by the sledgehammer, of the unimaginable painful reality, that Martin was dead.

She was so used to the alarm clock waking her up, with its annoying ping-ping at precisely 6.20, so she could be awake enough to hear radio 2's "thought for the day" at 6.25. This had been important to her as it was setting her up for the day ahead, giving her the encouragement and strength she needed to face it. Goodness knows how she had needed this daily crutch. She looked at the little alarm clock, " You have been a faithful friend for many years, but I think you have rung for the last time!" She turned the ringer off.

A million thoughts of the past went through her head, which for a change felt surprisingly clear and well rested.

"Now how am I going to attack this day?" She talked to herself. No one was listening, but it broke the unusual silence, "What shall I do first?"

*Well a cup of tea would be nice,* she thought. The room was warmish but with the window on the latch all night, the temperature in the room had rather dropped!

*I'll put the kettle on and top up the fires, then hop back into bed whilst I drink my tea. I can sit here and listen to the thoughts for the day and see what advice there is for me to gather. By then every where should have had a chance to warm up.*

She was good at giving herself pep talks and other bits of advice. She put on her slippers and dressing gown. That nice white thick fleecy one she'd had from her sister in law last Christmas. She sent her a loving thought every morning when she put it on. It was warm, soft and very comfortable, and she loved wrapping herself in it. Having no body else to wrap their arms around her, the soft warm fleece was the next best comforter.

She walked into the living room, the sun had not risen yet, but dawn was definitely breaking. It was still blowing, but a lot less than last night. There was sea spray on the windows! That was something she hadn't taken into account, salty sea spray, well hey-ho…every cloud has a silver lining.

'*I don't actually have a window squeegee, I must put that on my shopping list.*' She went to have a closer look. Beautiful crystals were edging the little opaque splats on the glass panes.

She filled the kettle with water, placed it on the AGA and listened to the noise it made. It did seem terribly noisy in the stillness. She went to the wood burner and found that there were still embers left from last night. Mr Morrison had been right, the peat turfs had certainly kept it going, albeit gently, all night. She put on a few bits of kindling wood and some bigger pieces on top, with the promise of a sunny day, by the look of it; there was no need to waste wood.

She would have to learn how to use the stoves correctly. But right now the house was cold and she could do with some warmth. Being cold only emphasised her solitude and being warm brought comfort, physically as well as mentally.

The rattle of the ash grate swamped the noise of the kettle, and as soon as she closed the doors the flames were already tickling the kindling wood. It was unusual to hear the kettle so clearly, and also the little crackles of the wood catching fire, and it made her pay even more attention to the quietness around her.

In fact if she hadn't been making any noises, it would have been silent. She sharpened her hearing as she poured the boiling water into the teapot, listening hard to any noises outside the house. She could hear the wind, and the thunder of waves in the distance. There were some little chirps of birds, but there was also something else, very faint, something that stirred childhood memories. Memories that made her feel warm and safe welled up inside her. What was it? She listened harder as pictures of Grannie's house and garden flooded into her mind. There it was again!

It was the sound of a cock crowing! She hadn't heard that sound for years.

"The best alarm clock in the world," she could hear Grannie's words from so very long ago. "It's useful, reliable and even good looking."

This was how the story of the birds and the bees had begun. Explaining how the little chickens arrived in the coop. She remembered that talk so clearly, now nearly fifty years on.

They were sitting in the warm kitchen, with hot chocolate and Grannie's freshly baked rolls. They had buttered them with lots of ice-cold butter, which quickly began to melt and sink into the warm bread. Whenever they had hot chocolate, which was quite often in the winter, she had occasionally been allowed to dunk the roll. The melted butter produced little yellow fat-pearls that would scuttle around on the surface of the chocolate. All she would have to do to get permission to dunk, was to catch Grannie's eye; who would then smile, give a nod and say,

 "Shall we?"

The candles were sparkling in her eyes and the smile was dancing round all the soft wrinkles in her face. *'I really think she enjoyed dunking as much as I did.'*

Funny, isn't it, how these warm and comforting memories from childhood are so chiselled into our minds, that by merely thinking about them or even just the smell of hot chocolate, can evoke such profoundly happy and safe feelings. Feelings we can take with us in our "backpacks" on the journey through our lives. The memories made her smile.

# 8

Here Vera was, a mature woman with lots of ups and downs behind her, but with the mere thoughts of Grannie's hot chocolate, she could still draw strength and happiness from the memories. It had been wonderful to be loved so unconditionally.

When she had gone through rough patches, and goodness knew there had been a few, thinking of Grannie always gave her the strength to carry on.

What an amazing bit of mental scaffolding.

Her thoughts went back to the dreadful day, when the maternity unit she worked at was closed down. It was shortly before Martin got poorly and she had to quit to look after him. It had taken the auxiliary nurse's suicide, for the management to realise just how bad things had got. That day was chiselled into her memory. It had started badly with driving into work early in the morning in the pouring rain. She had cursed that the car park was so far away and full of muddy potholes. She had felt so sorry for the poor cleaners, who had to mop up the muddy tracks from all the staff that hurried along the corridors to get to work on time. Elane, a lovely very experienced nurse and Vicky the auxiliary had been on night duty. They were nearly on their knees with exhaustion when Vera arrived, they said that they had hardly sat down all night. When Suzie then didn't turn up for the handover, they were all three worried, as she had never been late before.

The phone went as Elaine had just started the report. It was Suzie's husband calling in with the sad news of her death. The three of them had been so shocked. They had tried to get hold of the managers, but in vain, as they never answered their phones. The three women had felt completely helpless, and to top it, one of the patients suddenly started bleeding heavily. A code blue was called and suddenly the ward was full of people. Another consultant came to do a ward round in the middle of the mayhem, and a patient's bell was ringing and so was the phone. It was total chaos. When the emergency had been dealt with, Vera was just trying to get on top of the situation, writing notes at the desk. When a new CEO popped into the ward to say good morning.

That was the straw that broke the camel's back and Vera simply burst into tears. The very kind man just took her in his arms-what else could he do-as Vera broke down and sobbingly told him of the morning's happenings. Just at that moment one of the midwifery managers decided to turn up. She immediately got cross and started to tell Vera off. The CEO defended her-and invited the manager to go to his office straight away, as he informed her that she was sacked on the spot! He closed the maternity, and revised the whole set up. And the new refurbished maternity unit was reopened and called the Suzie, in her memory. To help everyone remember how important it is to respect the staff and give them a good work/life balance, and for all the staff to be heard and respected.

'*Memories, memories!*' she thought. How relieved she felt that this was all in the past, as she carried her tea and the transistor radio into the bedroom. The bed was still warm. Her program only lasted two minutes, but the thoughts it presented were always profound, and with careful attention she listened to the messages, which today were all about forgiveness and new beginnings.

'*How very appropriate,*' yes this message she had needed to hear. The new start had already happened, now it was up to her to forgive and forget. She was going to forgive and forget Keith Smith, and actually thank him for being so horrible, that the decision to move up here had been so easy to make. The reason why she ended up with a desk job, with him in charge, was because her nursing career came to a sudden stop, when she got the badly slipped disc, made so much worse by nursing Martin, and a NHS desk job was as close as she could get to anything to do with nursing.

Suddenly the rising sun blasted out of the sea, the water reflected the light into the bedroom where it now danced around. The energy was amazing.

She ran the bath, water was not a problem on the island, there was more than enough of it and the only problem to Vera was its colour. One thing had been to wash up in it last night, but to actually bathe in it was different.

The water on The Isle of Dogs in London had not been too clean either, except it always looked clean and smelt strongly of chlorine; it was just that when it dried it left a brown mark. She had never had the courage to investigate what the mark was, or indeed why it was brown. But rumour had it that the water in London had been through seven people before it came to you. Yuk, no wonder so many drank bottled water all the time.

Well the bathwater was indeed a beautiful golden brown, and once she had submerged herself in it, it was really lovely. It was incredibly soft, which she soon discovered as it was almost impossible to get the shampoo out of her hair. Well soap would have to be used in minute quantities from now on.

She aired the bedroom and made breakfast; the sun poured in through the windows, onto the yellow and white chequered tablecloth, and it sparkled in the glass candlesticks left on the table from last night. She laid the table properly, made some toast, and sat down with her shopping list.

Her mind was still clear and not at all jumbled. She could think straight, and was not hopping from thing to thing in her usual muddled way; this was new and felt calm and good. She wrote the things on the shopping list. Food for the weekend, there was not any need to write what, as she had no idea what there would be in the shop. But she also needed firelighters and stamps and batteries for the torch and the radio. She was going to write another list for all the things she would need in a big shopping spree, like extra beds for visitors and such like, and not to forget that window squeegee.

She opened all the windows and felt spurred on by the freshness of the chill air going through the house. Many of her belongings had been put into storage, and again her meticulous system of lists would benefit her, as she could now just call the storage firm and ask them to send box number so and so, as she needed them. She gave herself a mental pat on the back, thankful that she had been so organised. It really paid off.

Again the little key had fallen off and was lying on the worktop, she returned it to the nail. "How do you keep moving? It feels as if you want to get found."

At last she was ready to venture out and meet the day big time.

# 9

She noticed that the sun was not very high in the sky, although it was nearly 10.30. She would have to get used to telling the time differently now, as she was much further north and could no longer tell the time of day by the shadows or lights on certain buildings, as she had been used to.

The walk down to the post office was really enjoyable. She heard and saw several birds, some she knew and recognised, others made her realise that she would definitely need a bird watching book and a pair of binoculars, another few items for the big list.

A land rover came bouncing along the track and stopped by her. It was Beth the island's Nurse, who wanted to introduce herself and welcome Vera. They exchanged a few pleasantries, and Beth continued on her round. Vera thought how wonderful it must be to be a nurse here, and with regret she remembered the slipped disc that had put an end to her own nursing career. The back had recovered, thanks to Pilates and yoga which had strengthened the back and touch wood, it had been fine for some time, but she knew that she still had to be careful.

There was not much else but grass along the road. Road? Well! It was really more like a track of hard beaten earth, with a few stones embedded and a nibbled grass line in the middle. Sheep were grazing on the slopes on either side of the track. She noticed that they all had a different colour on their wool. Someone with a spray can had given them a little puff of paint probably so the various owners could identify them; she concluded. They seemed quite happy and content and didn't run away when she approached them, they just baaaaah'ed and carried on nibbling the grass whilst looking at her with their peculiar inquisitive eyes. Not brown warm eyes like a dog's, which made you want to stroke it. No, these eyes were cold and self-sufficient in a strange sort of way. She pondered whether it was the horizontal rectangular pupils that made them look so strange or maybe it was the yellow colour of their irises?

Some of the crofts had washing lines with gleaming white washing moving in the wind in the back yards. She turned and looked back at her little house. Arhhh didn't it just look so welcoming and cosy? The smoke was blown horizontally, as soon as it left the chimneys, by the strong breeze. She felt proud and confirmed to herself that the move to Strathsay had indeed been the right decision. It was really nice here with the crofts nestling in the soft green hills. She couldn't wait for this adventure to take off in earnest, there would be so much to experience and learn about.

The post office was busy with people coming and going. As she got nearer she could see several people waiting for the ferry. She couldn't quite believe that she had arrived on that very ferry not even 24 hours ago.

As she approached the building, a man stooped to come out of the shop door. His mustard coloured corduroy trousers were big and baggy and worn bald in the creases. His trouser legs were tucked into his home knitted socks, which were folded over above the sturdy walking boots. The home knitted pullover had leather patches on the elbows and had seen better days too, judging by all the repairs here and there. He was carrying a heavy rucksack and a leather satchel. He put them down as soon as he saw her,

"You must be the new lady in Harbour View." Smiling he stretched out both his big hands towards her and took her hand, which suddenly seemed so small, as it totally disappeared in his.

"I am Jimmy Lighthouse!" Was his friendly greeting. Well it was not difficult to work out where he lived.

"Vera!" She smiled up at his brown weather beaten face. His white bushy eyebrows thatched the deep set brown eyes and the many crow's feet made their way down his cheeks, and disappeared in the grey beard that matched his curly hair.

What a wonderful system! There was no need for surnames, you were known by your given name and which house you lived in.

"Vera!" He smiled as his big eyebrows flew up, surprised. That's the second time someone called Vera lives in Harbour View. My Grandmother was also called Vera. What a strange coincidence.

"So are you saying that your Grandmother used to live at Harbour View?"

"Yes, she sold it when she got old and moved in with my mother, in one of the harbour cottages over there. Her name was Anna." He pointed to the long row of terraced cottages. "The house has since been sold a couple of times, and the last owners were Londoners, they had it as their retreat. They did a lot of work to it and I understand that they have modernised it quite substantially."

"Well if you come by and want to have a look, a warm cup of tea will be awaiting you. You will always be very welcome."

"That is ever so kind of you, I would love to pop in on my way past one day, I walk to the shop at least once a week. A watering hole is always most appreciated. Now have a pleasant day won't you, we'll better be on our way."

They exchanged smiles and said goodbye. She felt weird. Her head was spinning and her heart was thumping irregularly; she went to sit on the bench outside the HUB. She sat there in the sun for a while, just quietly trying to let her emotions settle. Her heart was galloping. She felt a bit dizzy and light headed, and she was not quite sure what was happening. She just knew that she needed a few moments to let her mind absorb her emotions. What on earth happened when she shook his hand?

She'd looked into his brown, sparkling, warm eyes, and felt that she knew him. Felt as if she had known him all her life. She felt safe, as if this was exactly where she belonged. She could so easily just have snuggled up to him and let him embrace her with his big arms and let him protect her...What on earth was all this about? Something like this had never ever happened before. '*What's the matter with me? I must be tired.*' She tried to reassure herself as there was no way she could know him, nor know the house so all this dejavue '*must be my brain playing tricks on me*'.

She watched him as he picked up his heavy rucksack and swung it easily on to his back. He turned and looked back at her again-

"Are you all right?"

His frown showed that he was concerned. As she nodded reassuringly and smiled, he bent down and picked up the lead of the black Labrador who had been sitting so patiently waiting,

"Come on pal, let's go home," he said, and off they went. He had a shock of white gently curling hair and walked with a tall walking stick made from a forked branch. He had a strong stride, the dog was right by his side and he appeared to be talking to it, as it kept looking up at him as they walked.

Slowly her heart settled back to its old familiar rhythm as she sat there in the morning sun, just quietly. Some people walked past and greeted her with,

"Lovely morning!" and she answered back with a cheery

"It certainly is!"

And after a little while she took a deep breath, got up and went into the shop.

# 10

The little bell greeted her as she opened the door. Today the shop was busy; the ferry had brought much fresh produce yesterday, and being Friday today, there was a bit of shopping to be done for the weekend. Having no freezer Vera would have to learn to shop in a different way from now on - little and often rather than big and seldom.

At home she had been used to shopping online for most things, but in fact it was really nice to be able to actually see and touch what she bought. Reminding herself that she would have to carry it all back to the cottage, unless she was going to bother Mr Morrison.

It would make a big difference too that there would be neither friends nor family calling in for a chat or a meal now. When Martin had died, she had automatically still put two plates on the table, which used to make her cry in the early days. The portions were also much too big, but then she had a freezer and could just save leftovers for another day.

Vera told Mrs M that she had met Beth on the way. Mrs M told Vera that Beth had replaced the doctor and lived in the "Doctors House" at the edge of the village. The islanders had been a bit suspicious at first, but they had very quickly warmed to her. She was not only an extremely competent nurse but also a very clever and warm person, much loved and appreciated by all the patients, who had come into contact with her. The G.P. came over from the mainland once a week and saw the patients that needed to be seen by a doctor, but Nurse Beth on the whole managed all the day-to-day problems.

There were many people to say hello to and to introduce herself to, everyone was friendly and had something nice to say to welcome her. No one appeared to be too inquisitive or asked too personal questions. Space was the order of the day, and she supposed that this was island life: Very friendly and helpful, and at the same time accepting privacy.

She thought about it philosophically, there was a lot of space between the various dwellings, and she remembered a lecture she had attended some years ago.

The lecturer had explained how human and rat behaviour could be compared. He had said: "Put one rat in a cage, and it will be reasonably happy. Put two in, and they will begin to show signs of stress at times. Three, you are now heading for trouble, and as you increase the population the significant signs of stress, anxiety and illness gets more and more obvious. The same goes for humans too!" he had explained.

She had often thought of this phenomenon when moving about in London on the underground, on busses or trains. This was especially evident at rush hour when people were packed together, almost to suffocation point. Just observing people, there was no eye contact, no smiles and no conversation; people in London were in fact just like the rats, hyper-stressed with too many occupying that particular space.

But here, on the island, there was plenty of room and people could afford to extend themselves and made both eye contact and conversation easily. There was a new notice on the wall, colourful with big bold letters reminding people of tonight's ceilidh in the village hall.

The music would start at 8pm and there was a meal too which started at 18.00. Jamie Oliver's fish-pie no less was on the menu, and for dessert Jamaica ginger cake with vanilla ice cream, all for the incredible sum of £5.00 per person. Numbers to Mrs M. it said.

She asked if she could book a ticket, Mrs M reassured her that there was always room for one more at these gatherings.

"You can look forward to it, it is great fun, and you will meet most of the islanders, it is always a very popular evening." It sounded great and Vera was looking forward to it. This made tonight's meal easy! Then she would just have to get food for Saturday and Sunday.

Bacon, eggs, baked beans, tomatoes and mushrooms, bread she already had, another pint of milk, butter, some fruit, and of course the stamps, firelighters and batteries, would actually be all she would need for the weekend.

She found some washing powder, and noticed that all the cleaning products, and household liquids, were biodegradable. She asked about it and was told that every one here had a cesspit, for their wastewater, a private little sewage work. She had never heard of this sort of contraption, and was told that basically it consisted of two chambers, one which held all the solids, like coffee grains and small food scraps from the sink and washing up water, and everything from the toilet.

"So be very careful what you flush down the loo. The simple rule is as a matter of fact: Don't put anything in the toilet you haven't eaten first! " She laughed, "The next chamber holds only water, which then slowly syphons away into the ground, and is a fantastic fertiliser. Provided that you look after the cesspit and allow it to work to break down all the waste, and that means no chlorine and no harsh cleaning products at all."

So on the shelves there was no Dazz, Chlorine or Harpic toilet cleaner, nor was there any Flash…but there were all sorts of environmentally friendly and biodegradable products. Vera was sure that she would quickly learn to live with this new system if so many others were using it, so could she of course.

Mind you in London she had poured litres and litres of chemicals down the loo over the years, in the washing machine, dishwasher and down the drain in general. She had not given it a moment's thought that it could be harmful, but now that she had been informed otherwise, she was grateful for the new information and would change her ways. She had read of environmentally friendly issues, of course, but never thought it actually concerned her way of living. Living in London she had been so completely out of touch with her impact on the environment, that her own cause and effect on it had been easy to forget.

As she paid for her shopping and the ceilidh-ticket she asked if she could do anything to help tonight? Mrs M told her that no extra help was needed,

"Ye just turn up and enjoy it! It will be fun and ye'll meet near enough all the islanders. Don't wear anything too tight, or warm! Come and find me when you come tonight. I will introduce you to some people and you are welcome to sit at our table too if ye wish. See ye tonight dearrr." She smiled and went on to serve the next customer.

## 11

Vera almost hopped skipped and jumped all the way back to Harbour View, no not really but she certainly felt like it. When she crossed the little bridge, she stopped and looked down into the babbling brook. She got a strong urge to play pooh sticks, which she hadn't done for years. She promised herself that one of the first walks she would go on, would be to follow the little stream upwards to find where it came from. She tried to follow it with her eyes, but it was very difficult to see it properly. She would simply have to pack a lunch and a drink, and go exploring one day. She mentally added an ordnance survey map and a compass to the shopping list.

She decided as she walked home that she was going to write to Ruth and Michael, and formally invite them to visit her. She didn't have much in the way of bedding, but if they could bring sleeping bags, then she could always get some foam mattresses sent over from John Lewis, they would stack easily, and be no problem. She would write to them this very afternoon, and then she could post the letters tonight when she went down to the party. The letters could go back to the mainland on the ferry on Monday, all being well. There was no ferry service at the weekend in the winter half year.

Vera got her shopping put away, and finished unpacking the last few boxes. Then she went out to have a look at the woodshed and the potting shed. There were many useful things out there, like a lawnmower, an axe and a wood splitting tool, there was also the big tree trunk standing on the floor in the shed, to chop the wood on, it was there she had found the little key. *'I am going to have some fun with this, if I get really cross about something I shall come out here and chop wood, what an excellent punch bag!'* A very good way to get rid of pent up anger and she had just the word in mind to do it. Her former boss! His name would chop a lot of wood and she could feel it!

She found a piece that needed splitting, placed it on the trunk, grabbed the axe, felt the weight in her hand and arm, lifted it, and as she swung it forcefully into the log, she shouted: "KEITH SMITH!" The log split directly in two. *'Ahhh that felt good!'* She took another log, gave it the same treatment, and again shouted "KEITH SMITH!" as the axe flew through the air and bit deeply into the wood and the log split! Wow! This was great, what a tremendously powerful feeling.

Keith had been her boss for the last four years, and dear oh dear; he had caused her so much unhappiness and frustration. So many times she had gone home fuming because he had been so impossible, so unkind and often even nasty. He was going to chop a lot of wood for her and she was really going to enjoy it. This way she was going to get hot from the wood twice, the first time as she chopped it, the second time as it burned in the wood-burner. Brilliant!

She made a cup of tea and sat down to write to the children. Children! They were grown up now and had left home several years ago, but to her they would always be her children, however old they got.

The sun had moved round and was no longer shining on the dining table. The light here was so different to London, it gave her an amazing sensation of space around her. It was most likely because the water was reflecting the light, so you got double whammy. Thinking along those lines she suddenly thought: *'It is just possible that it would be economically viable to install solar panels on the roof, I will investigate the possibility on Monday.'*

As she drank the tea, she looked down to the harbour, which was getting more and more busy, and noticed that the ferry was almost arriving. Sitting there in her cosy room, watching the goings on, on the pier, she felt so content. There was really nothing she wanted for, she was just so happy to be here. She looked up at Martin's picture '*I just wish you had been here, Darling.*' And she also sent a very kind and grateful thought to her bee keeping friends. Thanks to them her hobby for many years had become her job. It was still much too cold to get the bees set up here, and also she would need to make some investigations as to what was actually growing here. Maybe she would need to plant bee friendly flowers and plants, maybe even fruit trees.

Tonight she could speak to a few islanders to see what they had growing near them. The hive in her back garden in London, was still there, the young couple, who she had sold the house to, had been very keen for her to leave it, and she had left information with her beekeeping friends to contact them in due course, to help them get started.

She wrote long letters to Lisa, Ruth and Michael and told them of her first impressions, and tried unsuccessfully to give a full description, which was of course completely impossible. Instead she told them that they would just have to come and see for themselves, as it was unimaginably wonderful. She gave them her new landline number, and said she couldn't wait to see them and share all this with them.

The letters neatly folded, she put them into the envelopes, wrote the addresses, and placed the first class stamp in the top right hand corner. And to finish, she wrote the name and address of the sender on the back. From: Vera, Harbour View, Strathsay, Scotland.

She put a bit of lipstick on and kissed the back of the envelopes! Thinking about her visitors she decided to ring to John Lewis and order two single beds and mattresses, and all the other things on the list straight away; she was very pleased to learn that they could be with her already on Monday in ten days time! She actually decided to buy new duvets and pillows and linen too whilst she was at it. It was enjoyable not to be penny pinching. Which was another great thing about her new life.

As that phone call had been so successful she decided that there is no time like the present, and rang to a solar panel firm and booked their representative to visit too. The secretary asked whether there might be others, who would be interested in some information and a possible site visit, if they were coming over to the island anyway.

Vera promised to put a poster about the visit on the notice board and for people to contact the firm directly, if interested. They agreed on a visit the first Friday in April, bearing in mind that there only was one ferry a day! It sailed on weekdays only in the winter half year; week ends too from May to September. At the moment she was not aware whether there would be anywhere to stay the night, otherwise the solar engineers would just have to be extremely quick and catch the ferry back as it returned to the mainland. It usually arrived around midday and left again at 15.00, which would certainly give them plenty of time to look at Vera's house, but others could be fitted in as well, especially if the firm could get hold of several surveyors.

The wood-burners needed another little feed, and she could do with some lunch too. As she was going to have a good meal in the evening, she only wanted a little something; she found some fruit and made a sandwich.

Poured herself a glass of juice and turned the radio on to hear the news.

Nothing much had happened which had any real interest, and she was pleased to turn it off, and enjoy the peace again. Sitting here in the warm room; she kept having déjavue.

Was this something she had experienced before...?

*'Is it because I have always wanted to live in a croft on an island? And have been daydreaming so much about it? Or have I actually been here before?* ' She pondered. The feeling was certainly strong, and she decided that she would not push it away, but just let it surface.

She sat on the sofa with her coffee, and closed her eyes. Suddenly her awareness was brought back to the room as the little key fell off its nail with a little tinkling sound.

"How strange!" She got up and went over to have a look - the string was intact, so how did it fall off? As she picked it up to hang it up again, she noticed again that it was warm. She went back to the sofa.

A very old memory from child hood came back to her. A band of Scottish Blackwatch Soldiers dressed in their highland regalia were marching, with drums and bagpipes. It had been overwhelming and very moving and strangely it had made her cry. She was not very old, but did remember that her mother had been very embarrassed at Vera's tears. Mum had yanked her arm. She was biting her teeth as she whispering told her to pull herself together and not cause a scene; for that very reason Vera had never touched the subject again.

Also she had noticed when she saw the ferry arrive at the island at lunch time, it had filled her with a feeling of a happy anticipation, which made no sense at all. She didn't know anybody who would arrive on it and she couldn't fathom where this excited feeling could come from.

There were so many new thoughts, feelings and experiences happening all at once. She decided that it would be best if she wrote it all down. It would make interesting reading for the ladies magazine.

Why had watching the dawn break so delicately and beautifully filled her with such pronounced energy and wellbeing? Where did Jimmy Lighthouse fit in to all this? Why did the ferry arriving fill her with joy? What was making the key move around? None of it made sense at all.

# 12

The walk to the village hall, which was situated just behind the post-office, was easy and enjoyable. It was still light when she set off as the sun wouldn't set for another hour.

The village hall was already full of people, when she got there. Outside was parked an old grey Ferguson tractor, several bikes, small mopeds and quad bikes. There were candles in all the windows. She could hear that the musicians were practising from the outside, and could see through the window that there was a real hustle and bustle inside. As she entered a wonderful smell of peaty smoke mixed with the spicy scent of whisky, filled her nostrils. Several people stood with a whisky glass in their hand, 'a wee dram!' as they called it here. They lifted it in a recognised greeting, nodded and smiled.

Vera spotted Mrs M and went over to say hello. She was busy putting a tablecloth on a table, but when she saw Vera she stopped and came towards her, with that by now so familiar and friendly, warm smile,

"Welcome, Welcome," she said. "Hang your coat in the cloakroom over there on the left, and then come and give Lizzie and me a hand." Vera went and took off her coat and the walking boots, a bit heavy and clumsy for a dance, and put on some lighter shoes. She wiped her cold nose, checked her appearance in the mirror, combed her hair, which had flown in all directions in the wind, which by now had finally settled down to just a mild breeze, and ventured a bit nervously back into the large hall.

There were many tables so many people were obviously expected. The musicians were standing on the little stage, which was at the end of the room, only a foot or so above the floor. They were having a break, each holding a whisky glass and having a laugh about something. Mrs M was in and out of the kitchen, from where the delicious smell of fish pie was wafting.

"Here you are," said Mrs M, "please put these flowers in these little vases and place one on each table." Vera was grateful for being given a job.

Lizzie was busy with the napkins and the cutlery, putting them in piles for the self-service, next to the plates that were stacked. Shortly everyone would walk past the serving hatch, having their portion put on their plate. Just like in school!

Lizzie and Vera shook hands, and introduced themselves. Well Vera did not need to introduce herself as such, as it was blatantly obvious that she was the new lady in Harbour View. She was the only new person in the village, actually on the whole island.

Lizzie came from the north-western side of the island, not far away from the lighthouse. She lived on Hill Farm, with her parents, an older brother and a younger sister. Lizzie was the driver of one of the mopeds. Vera told Lizzie that she was always welcome to call in if she came past. She had invited her second visitor! Lizzie was so impressed that Vera had moved all the way up here,

"You are very brave to move so far away. I've never been further away than going on the ferry to the mainland, and that is far enough away for me."

Vera was busy with the flowers, when someone gently tapped her on the shoulder. She turned a bit too abruptly, as she didn't know anybody well enough to be touched. Well who should stand there? Much to her surprise it was Jimmy with his big smile, and his arms by his side and slightly open palms facing her, in a surprised gesture.

"We meet again! Feeling better now?" He smiled. It really was as if she had known him always, and without thinking, she leaned into him, and let him embrace her, it just felt so incredibly natural. Mrs M walked past and remarked,

"Oh you two know each other, that makes the table arrangements easier. My son Peter has brought his girlfriend home for the weekend, so do you think you could sit at Jimmy's table instead of ours? Is that all right Vera? Sure you won't mind?"

No Vera didn't mind at all, she was actually pleased. She had to find out why he felt so familiar. As far as she knew she had never been here before, so how could it be?

They talked and talked during the meal, which was as delicious as she had expected. Jimmy drank beer and Vera enjoyed a glass of white wine. The conversation flowed so easily between them that Vera could hardly believe this was possible. It really was as if they were long lost friends, and had just picked up where they had left of the last time they met.

After the meal the musicians picked up their instruments again and the caller took the microphone and Jimmy helped her with the dances. It was a really good old fashioned fun evening, and she got introduced to so many of the islanders that it was impossible to remember who was who, and who lived where. Her head was positively spinning at the end of the evening, partly because of the twirling reels, and partly because of the white wine.

The Islanders were certainly very interested in her job as a bee-keeper and it was soon suggested that Vera should give a talk to them about bees and the importance of beekeeping. Which Vera was more than happy to organise. Mrs M suggested the second Saturday afternoon in April at 15.00 in the village hall.

Later as the evening drew to a close, the tidy up crew started to move tables and chairs. Everybody thanked each other for a lovely evening and started to drift home. Jimmy said that he would like to have the honour of walking Vera home,

"That is of course, if that's ok with you!" He hastily added.

Vera didn't mind at all, they were after all going in the same direction, so why not? They strolled towards Harbour View. The evening was milder as the wind had continued to drop; it was just past 23.00, but fairly easy to see in the moonlight. They walked side-by-side and Jimmy offered her his elbow. The gait suited them both perfectly. It seemed unbelievable that they had only met each other at lunchtime.

When they got to the white painted garden gate, they stopped, turned and looked down over the harbour. The reflection of the red light from the little lighthouse at the end of the pier could be seen on the water, and the lights were on in all the houses. It looked friendly.

"Your view is so different from mine Vera, all I can see is water. I live in one of the lighthouse cottages. One of those white painted ones with the shining black painted chimney pots, you know?"

No Vera didn't know that, she had never been to a lighthouse.

"It's very bleak out there on the northern rocks. I am so glad I have Sirius to keep me company."

"Who is Sirius?"

"Sirius is my lovely black Labrador, named after my favourite star, without him life would indeed be a bit lonely. He is really good company, he wakes me every morning by bringing me his blanket! Perhaps you would like to come to visit me and see where I live? Would afternoon tea be convenient tomorrow? We can walk round the promontory and fetch you, and show you our bit of the coastal path that goes right round the island. It's only a 45-minute walk, at a slow pace, 30 minutes if you stride out. What do you say? Oh, please say yes, I would really love to show you where I live, and for you to meet Sirius, I am sure you will like each other."

Vera thought that he was probably a bit lonely, and as they'd had such a great evening together, she accepted his kind invite without hesitation.

So that was then arranged and they thanked each other for an enjoyable evening and said good night. Vera walked the last few paces up to the cottage. Jimmy waited until she was safely inside before he walked on. She leaned her back against the closed door and took a deep breath. What an evening! She bent down and took of her walking boots, and hung up her coat.

She felt years younger, lighter, invigorated, and even buzzing. In her in-door shoes, she danced a few steps towards the worktop in the kitchen. Humming, she put the kettle on for her 'good night cuppa' and put some peat turfs in the wood burners. She went to the bathroom, and whilst brushing her teeth she looked in the mirror…*'HEY! I look different,'* she thought surprised, *'younger! My cheeks are red and my eyes are sparkling. I am just so happy!'* With the toothbrush still in her mouth, she smiled and the toothpaste froth dribbled down her chin into the sink-*'what a sight you are!'* She giggled.

A little later as she sat safely tucked up in her bed, warm and cosy, with the tea, she went over the events of the last couple of days. So much had happened in such a short space of time. It was unbelievable that this was only the second night in the new bed. She felt so at home already, so peaceful and so perfectly happy. How dramatically her life had changed. She folded her hands and thanked her maker for her incredible good fortune. She knew that from now on life would be good. She had finally found the place she had dreamt of, and felt as if she had indeed come home.

She was just about to turn off the bedside light when she noticed something on the windowsill. 'Not the key again?' She got up to investigate-it was that key, but how on earth had it got in here again? It was beginning to worry her, how could it move about like that?

She went back to bed and slid down under the covers, turned over and for the second night she slept a restful, deep and dreamless sleep.

# 13

The following morning she woke up aching all over. Her calf muscles in particular and the back and her arms were very sore. She felt as if she had been dragged through a hedge backwards.

"Ahhhhh." She sighed deeply and yawned as she slowly came to and stretched,

"I feel as if I have been pummelled in a rugby match. Pheww"

Then she sat up slowly and snuggled the warm cosy goose down duvet round her shoulders. The sun was already up. She looked at the alarm clock, blow me down. It was ten to eight!

'*My word I have had a real lie in.*' She was just reaching for the dressing gown, ready to jump out of bed, when she realised that there was actually no need to rush. It was perfectly all right just to sit here for a few minutes and just enjoy waking up. There was no bus to catch and no deadlines to meet.

She was here, right here. No rush, absolutely no rush! She breathed deeply and sighed with the realisation, and ahhhh this felt good, she sank back against the pillows. The room was pleasantly warm from the early morning sun helped along by the gentle background heat from the stove. She sat quietly and began to remember last night's shenanigans.

What an evening it had been!

She really hadn't enjoyed herself as much in a very long time. She had met so many really genuinely nice and kind people and they had all welcomed her into their group. She looked forward to getting to know them better, but again there was no rush.

She thought of how peaceful she felt, so at ease with the world, '*this is definitely the right place for me*', she concluded.

She folded her hands and closed her eyes, as grateful tears welled up and blurred her vision. They overflowed, and trickled down her cheeks. She remembered the old morning prayer from school: "I thank you Lord for keeping me safe this night, and praise you this morning and ask that you help me throughout the day. Amen"

She opened her eyes and dried the tears away with the back of her hand, sniffling she looked out over the sparkling water.

"Oh my goodness me! I have not been this happy for years…Righty-ho! no dawdling! Now lets get on with this day."

How was it the poem Houseman wrote went? The one that her Dad always recited? "Clay lies still but blood's a rover, life is aware and will not keep. Up lad for when the journey is over there will be time enough to sleep."

Energetically she threw back the duvet, so the top landed over the bed end, airing the feathers that had kept her so warm and cosy all night. Then swung the legs elegantly out of bed, fitted the feet neatly into the waiting in door shoes, and put on her dressing gown.

How on earth had the key got to the windowsill in the bedroom, she picked it up and put it in her pocket, she would return it to its nail in the kitchen.

Going past the bathroom she turned on the taps to run the bath. The golden water still surprised her as it began to fill the white bath.

In London she had only taken a bath very occasionally if she had come home late, cold or exhausted from work. In the mornings she always showered, it was quick and easy. Everything had to be efficient and fast then, but that was London, and this was Harbour View. A completely new and much more enjoyable lifestyle.

She hung the key up on its nail and boiled the kettle and made a pot of tea. She brought a mug into the bathroom, but before getting into the lovely warm golden-brown water, she filled the stoves again. It was easy to get into this new routine. The stoves were so efficient, and if today would be as mild as it promised to be, there would be enough wood until tomorrow in the basket.

Breakfast was delicious; toast and a boiled egg was just what she needed after all the dancing last night. She had been so grateful for the Caller's instructions, as she'd had absolutely no idea of what to do at the dances. It had been such fun; the memories of the evening flooded back, and made her smile.

After breakfast she got on with making the posters for the notice board. She found paper and colouring pencils and made a really eye-catching job of them both. One was for the bee-keeping information afternoon and the other one about the solar panels.

Then she hung a red cloth out on the brackets that held up the canopy over the front door, for Mr Morrison so he knew to call in. He could bring them to the post office and they could put up the notices, so as many could see them as quickly as possible.

The time had flown by whilst she worked on the posters, it was almost midday and it wasn't long before a toot-toot announced Mr Morrison's arrival. She went out to meet him, removing the red cloth on the way, and gave him the posters. He turned off the engine; put his elbow out of the window and tilted his head out too, as if he had all the time in the world,

"So you enjoyed last night." They laughed and reminisced. He asked what her plans were for the weekend, and she told him that she was waiting for Jimmy Lighthouse to walk over to fetch her.

"Archhh! What a coincidence-I'm actually on my way to him with this parcel, it arrived on the post-boat just now, it says fragile and deliver immediately, so I'm on my way to his house, why don't I give him a ring and tell him I will be delivering you too?"

She hesitated. She couldn't just turn up like that. What would he not think?

'Go on! Go and get your things, whilst I phone him." He was dialling the number, and she quickly returned inside.

*'I am not sure this is ok,-but he knows Jimmy better than I'.* She found a few of her own beeswax candles, and also a packet of Battenberg cakes, which was her favourite. She put on the sturdy boots and brought a rucksack with a torch, and her indoor shoes.

She put some peat turfs on the fires and left a light on in the kitchen, just in case it would be dark when she returned to the house. She locked the door, old habits die hard, and went down to the car. Mr Morrison was still on the phone to Jimmy, they spoke like very old friends. He was laughing, and finished the conversation with, "Well she's in the van now and we shall be with you in a jiffy, cheerrrioooohhh." He hung up and started the car.

"What did he say? I hope it is all right that you bring me over? You see I don't know him that well, we only met yesterday."

"Did you now!" He said without taking his eyes off the track ahead "I thought you were old friends the way you chatted last night. But I did wonder for two reasons. Firstly because I have known Jimmy for a very long time and know for a fact that he was born on this island and secondly he has never ever mentioned that he had a lady friend."

"No it is really weird, it feels like we are long lost friends and we have just picked up where we left it when we met last. He is just so easy to talk to."

"Ye have nothing to worry about with Jimmy, what ye see is what ye get. He is as solid as a rock and a kinder man ye will never find." Mr Morrison smiled, still keeping his eyes on the road.

The journey was really a bit bumpy, but the nature was fantastic. Mr Morrison pointed out the hills and the bays, and told her who lived where, and shortly when they rounded yet another headland, the northern rocks and the lighthouse came into view, it was spectacular! Painted white, it was standing all alone just on the rocks. It was true, it really was bleak here.

The lighthouse and the cottage were surrounded by a big wall, all white washed. Shining polished brass sparkled in the sunshine.

It was very impressive; everywhere was so well cared for. Vera paid special attention to the chimney pots, which were indeed painted shiny black, as Jimmy had said. He was right; the view from here was very different from Vera's. There was a bit of grass behind the lighthouse. In front of it was just bare rock going right down to the water, which stretched as far as the eyes could see.

Amazing! This view was breathtaking, Vera had never seen so much water. She found the fact that it was going on forever and ever and ever, scary and unsettling, just like looking at the stars at night, the enormity was quite overwhelming.

Jimmy had heard the van arrive and came out onto the huge granite front step, Sirius followed right behind him, wagging his tail. He was a beautiful, big strong dog, very calm and placid. Jimmy asked him to sit and wait by lifting his hand with a pointed finger, and walked down the five big wide granite steps to greet his visitors. He shook hands first with Vera and then Mr Morrison handed him the parcel.

"This is very intriguing, it is quite heavy, so it is obviously not something very, very delicate. Are you going to tell us what it is, or don't you know?"

"Oh, yes I know all right," Jimmy smiled, "would you have time to come inside and see when I open it, the kettle is just boiling. Vera and I are going to have a cup of tea, so why don't you join us?"

Mr Morrison excused himself, he would of course have loved to see what the parcel contained, but he had other parcels and post to deliver, so he'd better be on his way.

"Will you be walking Vera home or would you like me to come and fetch her later?" he inquired. Jimmy thanked him for the very kind and considerate offer, but he would actually love to walk Vera home and by the way Sirius could do with a good airing.

Mr Morrison left and they went into the cottage.

Vera's first impressions were how tidy it was. On the table in the kitchen stood a little vase with primroses with their delicately yellow almost white petals, and a few small twigs of pussy willow. Tiny, soft silky-haired and silvery-grey buds snuggled so closely to the chocolate brown bark, that it was hard to believe that they had come from the inside and weren't just glued on.

*'Excellent! There is willow pollen for the bees,'* was her first thought.

The cottage was bright and cosy. Jimmy had prepared a tray with teacups, and biscuits. When she gave him the box of Battenberg cakes, he looked at her and smiled,

His eyebrows lifted and the eyes peered over the glasses as he tucked his chin in, questioning.

"So…" he hesitated "you told Mrs M you were coming?"

"No, no." Vera bit her lip and shook her head; "I have actually brought them all the way from home. They are my favourite."

"So how on earth did you know about me and Battenberg's then?"

"I have no idea what you are talking about, it was the only thing I had in the cupboard apart from these little candles that I made."

"Candles?" Again his bushy eyebrows lifted in surprise, "and you made them yourself?"

She nodded and smiled. The kettle was boiling, to her relief he changed the subject and got up from the chair.

"What sort of tea do you like?"

"I am not fussy at all, as long as it is hot and wet I drink it as it comes. Having worked as a nurse, you learn to be grateful for any cup of tea."

He scalded the teapot, and then poured the boiling water directly onto the tea leaves, and placed it under a colourful knitted tea cosy.

*'He makes proper tea! How delightful!'*

"So are you going to tell me why Battenbergs are so special?" She laughed a little uneasily, not sure if she was getting into deep water, by asking what all the secrecy was about.

Jimmy came to the table with the tray,

"I am so thrilled you have come to see us, and what a lucky thing that the parcel should arrive at the same time", he fetched it and brought it to the table, and opened it carefully. As he removed the paper he started smiling, the smile became a giggle, and when the inside was eventually revealed, he laughed out loud.

The parcel contained Battenberg cakes, ten boxes of them! Then they both laughed! The uneasiness had melted away; they could talk as easily as yesterday again.

"I love Battenberg cakes, and now I have discovered I can have them delivered directly. You see I normally fetch them myself at the post office, this is my only vice, I simply can't get enough of them." He looked like a child that had been caught out.

"Don't you worry Jimmy, your secret is safe with me as I am just as crazy about them."

He picked up the little yellow candles, turned them in his hands and brought them up to his nose,

"Mmmm the smell of proper beeswax candles takes me right back," he said, breathing deeply through his nose, closing his eyes, letting memories flourish.

"Mmmm, and you made them yourself?"

"Yes, I kept bees in London."

"Old Adam kept bees, but he passed away, let me see, must be about twenty years ago now. All his beekeeping stuff is still in the shed, maybe we can look at it one day?"

"Who is Adam?"

"He was my uncle, my mum's brother. He was one of the lighthouse keepers. There used to be three of us here, Adam, Rory and me. "

Vera reminded him of the reason for her coming to the island, and how important it would be to get the bees back. She was hoping there would be many who would like to become beekeepers.

"Well, I have absolutely no idea where to start with it all, but I would be keen to learn." Jimmy was enthusiastic.
Vera was pleased she had her first interested person; hopefully more would come forwards once the beekeeping poster was seen on the notice board

After the tea, he wanted to show her the lighthouse. She was so impressed and commented on how gleaming all the brass was everywhere. The lantern and the foghorn were being controlled by radio from The Northern Lights Board in Edinburgh. Which meant that the hourly patrols were not necessary anymore, which also meant that Jimmy could now sleep all night. It had taken years to learn to do that, and even so he would still get out of bed and check things over, the old routine was so ingrained. Sirius was so used to his master wandering about at night that he dutifully left his basket and followed Jimmy about on his checking patrol, before they both returned to their beds to carry on sleeping.

As the lighthouse was so remote, and so difficult to get to, Jimmy had been allowed to stay living in the cottage, where he had lived for the last 42 years. It was a lifestyle that was not easily changed. He had started as a boy helper when he was 15 and left school, and had been there ever since; he was eventually promoted to senior lighthouse keeper.

In the old days, the lighthouse crew stayed on duty for months on end. One had to be incredibly tolerant, as the slightest sniffle or irritating habit being it a cough, or a scratch or the way someone blew their nose, or made tea, in the end could make sane men go round the bend. It was not easy to be cooped up with each other for weeks and weeks on end.

They had to be quite self-sufficient so they grew and made a lot of things themselves. Composting had been the order of the day and nothing went to waste. They kept goats for milk and chickens for eggs, and there were others on the island that had sheep and livestock, so life on the whole had been pretty good. Old Adam had kept bees and made honey and candles, hence Jimmy had recognised the scent.

And of course they could also socialise, a bit, but the 45 min walk sometimes prevented outings, especially in bad weather and also in the winter half year when it grew dark so early. The short winter days meant that they had time for many indoor activities; most of the men were very skilled in many crafts. Knitting was one of them, woodwork another, painting and poetry would also pass many hours. And of course in the summer the kitchen garden took up a lot of time. Making jams and preserves, making wine and pickling vegetables, all in preparation for the long isolated winter months.

The green house had to be seen to, as well as all the upkeep and daily routines of the actual lighthouse. They were never bored. They took watches and turns in cooking and baking, but now Jimmy was living here alone, he couldn't really do it all. So the kitchen garden had shrunk, and he didn't keep chickens anymore. He relied on Mr Morrison delivering most of the heavier goods, but even so Jimmy did the walk to the shop at least once a week, when the weather allowed. He was self-reliant and only asked Mr Morrison's for his help when it was absolutely necessary.

Vera understood that Jimmy could do with some help; there was definitely much too much upkeep for one person to see to here. The place was massive for just one person. She wondered if The Northern Lighthouse Board helped him at all?

Well, he hadn't actually asked for any help, but he could see that perhaps it was necessary. Vera suggested that they could write a letter and see what they would say. They agreed that they would do that together one day next week.

Vera told him of the solar panels she was hoping to install. Did he think N.L.B. would be interested in installing some at the lighthouse? They could perhaps ask Mr Morrison if he would mind bringing the surveyors to the lighthouse when they came to Vera's in April. Jimmy thought it was a brilliant idea, and that they could include this in the letter. N.L.B. would probably be interested in investing in Green Energy. A penny saved is a penny earned- so the old saying went.

Time was flying, they felt good in each other's company, as the sun was getting lower, they thought it best to get on the way to get Vera home, otherwise Jimmy and Sirius would have to walk back in the dark.

They walked easily, sometimes talking, sometimes just appreciating the company in silence; it was good just to be together. They passed comments on the view as they walked, the fresh air, the birds they saw, and they soon got back to Harbour View. Vera quickly put the kettle on, and they had a quick cup of tea. Sirius seemed at home in the kitchen. He had found himself a cosy corner at the wood burner, as if to say this is my place, I like it here. Vera and Jimmy sat at the dining table drinking the tea, admiring the view. Jimmy was very complimentary about the whole cottage, it had certainly changed since his Grandmother lived there. Jimmy used the bathroom before setting off again.

"Under-floor heating eh? What a delightful luxury. Well I suppose I had better be on my way. Thanks for a lovely afternoon, it has been great spending time with you."

It felt a bit lonely when he left. She watched them as they trotted away together until they had disappeared round the headland.

What now? She felt lost. It was getting late and the sun would soon be setting, the sunset was spectacular. She looked for things to do. The wood burners needed a feed. She had better go and fill the basket before it got dark and think about some supper. The long walk had made her quite hungry. She could have asked Jimmy for dinner, but then he would have had to walk home in the dark, that would have to wait until the days were longer. She brought the wood in, the wood burner had nearly gone out, she hadn't noticed as the sun had been shining and kept the cottage warm.

The wood quickly started crackling and the flames soon danced again behind the windows, spreading a warm glow as the light really began to fade outside. She decided to make a baked potato in the Aga, and have it with some baked beans and a bit of bacon. The bacon was quickly done in the oven, she had to keep opening the door to check on it, as there were no cooking smells, because the oven vented to the outside.

It had been such a lovely day. She lit some candles and sat down on the sofa waiting for her meal to finish cooking.

*'Actually, I think I'll have a glass of red wine.'* She poured a glass and sat down again listening to classical music. She was so lucky, what more could she possibly ask for, this was just heaven. Well one thing would have made it better, if Martin had been here! She looked up at his picture on the mantelpiece, and lifted her glass to him. She could almost see him give her a wink.

# 14

On Sunday morning she sat in her bed and watched how the lead grey night sky met the sea on the horizon. It was being pushed away by a band of golden yellow that grew and grew. It almost looked like it was a battle between darkness and light. As the sun came nearer the horizon, the whole under side of the leaden heavy clouds were ablaze. Suddenly the sun rose powerfully out of the sea. Within seconds it was so bright that she couldn't look directly at it. It didn't last! Soon the clouds hid it again.

She went to put the kettle on and give the wood burner a top up. She was very well aware that the wood in the shed had to be used sparingly, as it would be very hard work to saw and chop the next load. She was just running the bath, when she heard the phone ring. She turned the water off, and went to answer it. It was Ruth.

"Morning! Sorry to ring so early, I didn't wake you did I? How are you getting on Mum?"

"Good morning Darling, no not at all, I am just running a bath whilst the kettle boils. What's up poppet?"

"Well, I am so excited Mum, and that's why I'm ringing, I've managed to get some extra days off as I'm ahead with my coursework. How would it suit you if I come and see you on the first Friday in April and stay until Monday?"

"That would be so lovely darling, I've actually sent you a letter yesterday to invite you. I shall really look forward to that! What a lovely surprise Ruth, bring your walking boots and practical clothes, especially something warm. Will you be coming on your own or are you bringing a friend?"

"No this time I am just coming on my own Mum. It will be nice for you to show me all the new things around you, and we shall have lots of time to chat. Oh I really can't wait. You sound so happy Mum and it seems so long since we've had some 'just you and me' time."

"Yes that is true." She was right; time in London had been so pressured for both of them.

"Good Mum, I'll get on and book the tickets and then we'll see each other really soon. Let me know if there is anything you would like me to bring, ok?"

"Oh! Just before you go Darling," Vera suddenly remembered that the surveyor was coming that day too, "I have arranged for some solar power engineers to come and see if it a good idea to put photovoltaic cells on the roof, and they are coming that Friday too, just so you know."

She told Ruth to travel lightly as there would be a half an hour's walk slightly up hill, to reach the croft,

"So wear your strong boots" the mother came up in her again. They rang off and Vera went back to the bathroom, turned the water back on and started to brush her teeth at the sink. How exciting! She was already having her very first visitor. She looked at her smiling self in the mirror. Pleased that she had already ordered beds and bedding and that is would be delivered Monday next week, so it would all be ready when Ruth arrived in April.

She brought the radio into the bathroom and listened to the Sunday service, which today came from a church in Wales. They sang her favourite hymn, Praise thee, oh thou great Jehovah, and she sang out loud with the wonderful male choir, *'if anyone could hear or see me now they would surely have a good laugh,*' she thought as she could see the comical side of the situation.

In the bath, after the service, she made plans for Ruth's visit. It was so relaxing lying here in the amber water. She could feel the water was re-energising her with all its minerals. She wondered if her skin might turn brown if she lay in the water long enough. That thought made her smile.

On a small notice board, outside the post office, there had been a small plastic container with maps of the island, and she had brought one home. She went looking for it after the bath, and sat down at the table with it, whilst having breakfast.

Being Sunday she always had coffee instead of tea. She made it in the little cafetier and put the tea cosy over it to keep it warm.

Studying the map she could clearly see the lighthouse on the northern end of the island. It stated on the map that to the west there were some cliffs with puffins, how exciting! Vera had only ever seen pictures of these fantastic birds with their colourful beaks. Out there on the western cliffs there was also a teahouse marked too. A good place to go for a day's outing when Ruth came. She also spotted the little brook, where she had felt like playing pooh sticks the other day, she could see that it came from a little tarn in the hills.

On the east coast there were many sheltered coves and sandy beaches, there were nesting places for many different birds in that area. Entrance was therefore restricted in some places at certain times of the year.

The village spread out on either side of the jetty. She noticed the church, which looked amazing situated on the hillside, majestically looking out to sea. It seem to be watching over the village.

The leaflet also informed her of the library bus and the Bank of Scotland's visits, once a fortnight they would arrive on the ferry and park at the jetty.

Well she wouldn't make too many plans for Ruth's visit, it would just be nice to take the days as they came, and just relax together. Perhaps it would be an idea to get some housework done today.

She decided to hoover and clean upstairs first. It was a really easy house to clean, and she enjoyed getting it all done. It was very satisfying to have been to every corner getting to know the house inside and out.

# 15

One afternoon there was a knock on the door. Vera was quite surprised, and went to answer it. It was the nearest neighbours, Karl, Emma and Simon. They thought they would just call by with the island's welcome tradition: cake, dram and peat...to say hello and to welcome her to the island. They lived just round the bend and their house was called "Hill Side".

Vera put the kettle on and invited the little family to take a seat. They commented on how cosy it was in her house, and hadn't she done well to get so organised so quickly.

Simon, who was five, and a bright little boy. He felt at home straight away, even though Vera didn't have any toys for him to play with. He was very content just to sit on the sofa with mum and dad and talk.

What a lovely little family! Emma was expecting their second baby in June, and she both looked and felt really well. They were artists, Karl was a sculptor, carving wood, and Emma made patchwork. They were also very keen kitchen gardeners. They had chickens, and often had eggs for sale. Could this be where she'd heard the cockerel crow from?

They had seen the notice about beekeeping and commented on Vera's artistic skills. She played it down, but both Karl and Emma thought she had real talent. They were very interested in the beekeeping talk.

They talked a bit about keeping chickens; Simon told Vera how he enjoyed going out in the morning to collect eggs before going to school. He told her that there was actually a chart in the school where they kept a tally of how many eggs he and a few other children were managing to collect. Some had to be left to be allowed to develop into chicks too. So they did have a cockerel! The mystery was solved, one day she would tell Simon about her grandmother's chickens.

They were potentially interested in beekeeping, maybe not to have hives themselves, but would certainly like to learn more about it. They asked if Vera had spoken to the headmistress in the school? They were sure that she would very much welcome a talk by a proper bee-keeper for the school children. If Vera was agreeable could they put her name forward? And of course she was. Simon had started in the school only this January, and was so excited about it. He told Vera about his teacher, and showed her how many letters he could recognise already, AND that he could also spell his name: sir, eye, meh, oh, neh.

He was very proud, and Vera praised him. She'd liked him straight away. And he liked her! That was so obvious. He was relaxed and chatty. Vera had always got on fantastically with children. They seem to feel at home with her straight away. In London she could never go and sit in the park without some children finding her and starting to chat with her, it had been quite embarrassing at times. Sometimes she'd felt she was like the pied piper from Hamelin.

Their house had always been the common playground for all the other kids. They had felt at home, and when they became teenagers they confided in her, she'd had countless hours of cups of tea and kitchen roll on the table for the mopping up of tears. Listening to their worries and troubles, and to the stories of how their parents didn't understand them, of how the girl's mothers would surely kill them if they knew this and that. She was a real confidante for them all. Some still kept in touch even after all these years.

Emma and Karl commented on how amazing it was that Simon had bonded with Vera so quickly. She offered to be "reserve grandma" as she had no grandchildren; and the offer was gratefully accepted as the real grandparents were too far away, so Simon didn't have any regular contact with them. Vera said to Simon that they would have to make a little bag of things he liked, so when he came to visit he'd have some familiar things to both play with, read, do colouring with and so on, as she had absolutely nothing in the house at the moment that could amuse a five year old.

The little family said goodbye and went on their way home, promising to be in contact, as they walked by everyday to and from school. Vera was very pleased to have made friends with them, and told them that they were always welcome to call in for a cuppa and a chat.

Simon hopped, skipped and jumped down the path to the track waving good-bye, whilst humming a little tune, smiling and brimming with happiness. Mum and dad linked arms as they walked behind him at a much slower pace; he just had so much energy. Vera stood in the door and watched them as they disappeared round the bend; she smiled as she went back in side and closed the door.

She made a note to herself to remember to contact the storage firm to forward box 30 and 31, which contained all her beekeeping gear. She would also contact Thorne's the beekeeping suppliers in Wragby in Yorkshire and see whether she would be able get a special discount if there was enough interest in the bee keeping. All this went on tomorrow's to-do-list.

She loved her simple little bedroom, and she had already got used to sleeping with the windows open and not drawing the curtains. Now she found it almost impossible to think that she used to sleep with the windows closed and even locked too. She used to have the heating off and curtains drawn, now the thought almost made her feel claustrophobic.

Last thing she went round the house, putting turfs in the stoves, blowing out the candles, going to the bathroom whilst the kettle boiled for the good night tea. She put on the pyjamas, found her book and turned in.

It was heavenly to get into the bed; she turned out the light, and just sat and watched the buoys blinking, and the sweep of light from the lighthouse. She was thinking of Jimmy out there on the rocks with Sirius. She drank the tea, and was so glad that she had had the courage to pull up the tent pegs, what a blessing it had been that this opportunity had come her way. Tomorrow would be another exciting day, and she wondered what it would bring.

## 16

The following Monday came faster than she had anticipated. She knew from experience that when you were looking forward to something, time always dragged. It was a bright morning and she knew that she had to be organised early, as the delivery van would arrive on the ferry. She would go down to meet the van and guide them to her house. She presumed there would be two men in order to carry all the things.

She had a quick shower and got dressed, whilst the kettle boiled. It was interesting how quickly she had hopped back into her old busy morning schedule and completely forgot the no rush promises she had made herself.

In the outside shed she had found an old fashioned deck chair, with the most fantastic stripy material beautifully tacked on to the frame. I am going to sit out here if I get time today, with a nice cup of tea. *'If I get time!' How often had she not said that sentence to herself in London. Now she was definitely going to MAKE time for that cup of tea.'*

She also found a peg-bag hanging on a big 6-inch nail. *'good timing it is just what I needed, it saves me rummaging in the boxes.'* Being Monday she had stripped the bed and had put the bedding and the towels in the washing machine.

In the potting shed there were lots of small pots and trays for planting seeds. '*Well I suppose it is that time of year again,*' she thought. She used to have a few herbs growing in the garden, but here there was room for some more exciting vegetables and maybe even fruit bushes. And roses, she would definitely get some roses delivered, Martin had loved roses, he didn't like gardening, but he adored roses.

As she went back into the kitchen the perfume of the boil wash and new washing powder greeted her. '*What a pleasant smell,*' and once more another childhood memory popped up. She put the kettle on and stood still just watching it whilst the memories slowly surfaced.

The warmth in the kitchen and the smell of the clean washing took her back years. Mum had a long washing line in the garden between the apple trees. A long pole helped to raise the line high up so the big bed sheets could blow easily in the wind, 'dried by the sun ironed by the wind' she used to say. It was the smell of the washing that stirred that memory.

Vera was already looking forward to ironing the sheets; they would surely smell really lovely.

She had not been drying clothes outside in London, even though she had a garden; she had always used the tumble dryer. It had been so much easier to put the clothes straight in there directly from the washing machine. Occasionally she had dried things in the garden, but the whites always had tiny specks of black, that made them look a bit grubby, although in theory they should have been clean. '*If the clothes absorb this, I wonder what our lungs look like*', she had wondered and had refrained from line drying.

Never mind! She was not going to worry about pollution in London now, she was here, the air was fresh and the washing machine would surely do a brilliant job and then she would enjoy the freshly laundered clothes. The AGA would also be good for airing them on too.

She could see the ferry in the distance. In a little while she would get ready to go down to meet it. She brought a soapy cloth with her to wipe the line before she hung the clean bed linen on it. Much to her surprise she found that it was clean. With the washing pegged out, Vera stood for a moment and just enjoyed watching the clean washing moving gently in the breeze on the line. She was pleasantly surprised, as she didn't think that the golden water and the ecological washing powder would do a very good job, but it had, and she was very pleased with the result.

Then she made that long awaited cup of tea and brought it and a flapjack out to the deckchair. Sitting here she could keep an eye on the ferry, it was actually not moving quite as fast as she had first anticipated. She cupped her hands around the warm mug. It was bright and the sun was shining, but warm it wasn't. She drank up, put the chair away again and went in to get ready. Rinsing the mug she found the little key on the draining board. *'How did that get over here?'* Again it felt warm.

"I really don't know how you can keep moving about like this, it's as if you have a life of your own. You really want to be found all the time don't you?" She was puzzled and hung it back on its nail.

It was a lovely walk in the sun and the fresh sea breeze down to the jetty; the waves were gently lapping the shore. The grazing sheep went about quietly and undisturbed. They never ceased to amaze her; they were such patient and undemanding creatures, she noticed that a couple of them had new born lambs.

Several people waited on the pier and they stood together in a little group. They were talking about how lucky they were with the weather,

"It's not been this good for a very long time, the weather is usually dricht this time of year, but since you have arrived it's been unusually good." They said and smiled to Vera. She joined the group and some asked if she had enjoyed the evening last Friday. They were all so friendly and she knew she had been introduced to all of them the other night in the hall, but she couldn't remember their names, there had just been too many of them. She asked politely to be reminded once more. She also asked if anybody had had time to look at the notice board to see her notices? Those who had seen the posters commented on the attractive colours she had used and said how they had really caught their eye.

She was pleased to hear their comments, and left it at that not wanting to appear to be pushy. People would make up their own minds in their own time, but that some showed interest in beekeeping, really pleased her.

The ferry arrived, offloaded its cargo of people and boxes and vans. The John Lewis one stood out a mile. She overheard some people wondering what they'd be bringing and to whom.

She went to the driver and said hello. He was alone so she hopped in to the passenger seat, and together they drove the little distance up to the house. The driver was extremely complimentary, about the island and her home. He enquired how long she had lived there and was so surprised to hear that she hadn't even been there three weeks yet.

They helped each other empty the van and carried the mattresses, the pillows and duvets up the stairs. The new towels and the linen she put in the kitchen ready for a trip in the washing machine prior to being used. He praised the cottage, it was so homely and welcoming, he smiled looking around.

Vera offered him some lunch, which he gratefully accepted. Just a mug of soup and some bread, and to finish a lovely cup of coffee, which she made with freshly ground coffee beans in the cafetier, and a flapjack.

The coffee was new to the driver as he was used to instant coffee powder, but he was very appreciative and he said that he was definitely going to make coffee like this in the future, now Vera had told him how easy it actually was.

He had to be at the ferry in good time before departure, so the time was quite short. He gave her his name and said that he would be very happy to volunteer to come again, as he was a very keen bird watcher and had never been to Strathsay before and would certainly not mind returning, and perhaps even spend some more time on the island. He wondered whether there was any bed and breakfast accommodation available. Vera didn't know that but said that she would investigate so they exchanged e-mail addresses. He thanked her very much for her hospitality and went back to the ferry.

She went back indoors and started arranging things upstairs. Ruth would have been very happy just sleeping on a mattress, but now she could sleep in a proper bed. She put the beds in an L shape, and moved the little bedside table from the un-occupied side of her own bed, into the corner between the two beds, and put the bedside light on it. It looked very cosy once she was finished. She put a blanket and some cushions on the empty bed, having rolled the duvet into a sausage up against the wall, it would be a nice place to sit and watch the stars at night, or even have a good night chat with

Ruth, before they went to sleep. She could feel the happy anticipation of the impending visit bubbling up inside her.

The afternoon quickly went, she got the dry washing inside, folded it all neatly, and decided that she would iron it all straight away. It did indeed smell fantastic! The sun was setting on yet another day, it was unbelievable how fast these days passed by and how much she managed to achieve and get done. She had been so pleased to put the freshly ironed linen away in the cupboard. She looked longingly at the bed as she went past it. She had also been very surprised how soft the towels had become without the use of fabric conditioner.

She then made a nice dinner, poured a glass of wine and lit the candles and sat down at the table. The radio was still tuned to classic FM. There was a pleasant temperature in the room, as the wood burner was gently smouldering on a large log.

She was just enjoying the peace and quiet, it had been a busy day, and she was really looking forward to Ruth's visit. Whilst eating her dinner she was thinking about what she needed to prepare food wise before Ruth arrived. It would probably be a good idea to bake a cake and make some freshly baked rolls and put them in the little freezer. Perhaps even make a quiche or two, so they had something to bring on a picnic, if that was what they decided to do. Maybe they would just stay in the cottage, do a bit of gardening perhaps or maybe just sit in the sun and chat. Ruth was keen on water-colours, and always had her sketchbook with her so she might be content just to sit and sketch and soak up the atmosphere here.

Most importantly Vera wanted Ruth to experience "the absolutely no rush" way of life the island offered. Rushing was not allowed; and it had become Vera's new motto.

She better start another shopping list for food for that weekend. Once she had the menu sorted it was quite plain sailing. Fortunately Ruth was not very fussy about food, she would be happy with just about anything.

So out came pencil and notebook, and she wrote a to do list. Better make some soup for the surveyors too, she added. Vera had not cooked on an Aga before, and although it wasn't difficult as such, there were certain things she needed to be aware of and learn to adjust to. It was easy to burn food in the ovens. As they vented to the outside, there were no cooking smells to alert you that things had had enough. So a timer was essential.

You also can't turn the hot plates on or off, nor up or down, instead you have to move the saucepans in and out on the hotplate, to regulate the temperature. There is a boiling plate and a simmering plate, so saucepans had to be moved about for that reason too. Some of her friends that had an AGA absolutely swore by it and would never be without theirs. They said it was the soul of the home. But truth be known it is an acquired skill to learn how to cook on it she realised, but it would probably not be more difficult than she could manage.

She thought she would make something with fish, and also a roast dinner of some sort, with roast potatoes. Ruth would really appreciate that, she was absolutely sure. Family Sunday roasts had been a very important time for them all.

It was getting dark; she cleared up after dinner and made the usual cup of good night tea, which she brought to bed with her. Sitting in the warm bed, reading her book she soon felt drowsy. In London it had always taken some time for her brain to simmer down. Some nights it never happened and she was tossing and turning all night long, only to get up feeling exhausted the next morning.

Oh what a treadmill the London life had been, and how scary that she hadn't even noticed how she had got more and more stressed and wound up. It was not before now that she noticed how good she was feeling, that she realised how bad she had felt these endless years since Martin died.

# 17

The following day went with washing the new towels and bedding and doing the ironing and making more lists. She was very organised. She had a ring binder where she had all the lists in alphabetical order. It was her way of keeping it all under control. She could easily flip back and forth and check on things.

Jimmy rang and asked if he could pop by on the way to or from the post-office, he was expecting another delivery on the ferry! Of course he was more than welcome, and Vera suggested that he called in on the way back. She would make some tea and they could test that the cakes had not gone off! Ha-ha.

Over tea she talked to Jimmy about Ruth's visit, and showed him the nice guest bedroom she had made. Jimmy was really impressed, but said in future when she had things like that to do, never hesitate to ask for help, as he would be delighted to help with anything. Vera thought it would be really nice for them to meet up over the weekend; and asked if he might like to come over for a roast dinner on Sunday. Which he was delighted to accept, and Vera said,

"Please bring Sirius, Ruth is a vet student and she loves dogs."

She asked what his favourite roast was. Jimmy said that he rather liked a slow roasted shoulder of lamb. Automatically he licked his lips at the thought, "..with rosemary and lots of garlic, roast potatoes, peas, carrots and mint jelly?" she butted in.

"Oh yes! That is exactly right." He smiled, and swallowed as he could feel his mouth watering. Vera laughed and said she would do her best to cook something nice.

"And what about Yorkshire puddings?" She added. "Oh yes not to forget them either!" Jimmy smiled. "By the way Jimmy, where do you get your meat from? I noticed they didn't sell meat in the post office."

"No, you will have to go to Mr McBurn the butcher, he is not too far away. Go past the post office, he is on the right just after the small enclave of white painted cottages. You can't miss the window; he has such a beautiful awning over it."

# 18

The next morning she woke to spring rain, which was steady and gentle, a real drenching with no end in sight. The clouds and the horizon had merged. The visibility was so poor that she could just see the jetty, but only just. She decided to phone the post office to speak to Mrs M about the beekeeping afternoon,

"We could make things with honey in, have you got any recipes?" Mrs M asked. Vera thought she might have some somewhere, and would certainly Google some, if she couldn't find them.

The meeting was arranged for Saturday the 14th of April at 15.00. They would start with tea and cake first, and then Vera would give a presentation, and show them her veil, smoker, gloves and hive tools and an empty beehive. Mrs M would put the date on the notice board, and also take the numbers, so Vera did not have to worry about that at all.

She then telephoned beekeeping equipment suppliers Thornes in Wragby in Yorkshire and told them about the reason that she had moved to Strathsay; and as she was arranging the beekeeping event, there was a potential for several new customers. They offered to either come to the event, with lots of supplies, or just send some brochures. Vera was very grateful for all their help, and said she would be in touch when she had some more information.

She then rang to butcher Mr McBurn, introduced herself as a new customer, and asked if it would be possible to order some meat for the first weekend in April. She would like a large shoulder of lamb and some beef mince to make cottage pie. Vera wanted to know how she was going to cook the lamb, confessing her lack of knowledge of cooking on the AGA.

"Oh! You're lucky! An AGA is absolutely perfect for slow cooking lamb, well any roast for that sake. You just put it in the roasting oven for about 20 minutes, and then cover it with tin foil, and put it in the simmering oven for as long as you like and I can tell you, you will never have tasted meat like it! And the same goes for the minced beef, brown the onions in the dish first, then ad the meat, brown it well. You can then either do it in the oven or on the boiling plate, once browned, add stock, season, cover and bang it in the simmering oven, again for as long as you like, the longer, the better actually. Just be careful you don't forget it, ha-ha-ha, it is surprising how easily that is done. Many a good meal has been forgotten in an AGA. Would you like the meat delivered?"

"No, no, thank you! That's not necessary, I'll be going to the post office for my other bits and pieces, when I fetch my daughter from the ferry at midday, so I will pop in Friday morning if that is convenient. But thank you ever so much for the offer."

"Goodbye then, I look forward to seeing you then, Cherrrrrriooo"

"By-ee." Vera hung up. Then she went on to the shopping list. She sat down with a cup of tea and put on her thinking hat. She brought out the list she had made earlier, added a few bits and pieces, writing out the menu for the long week end, and then rang Mrs M, so she could order in the things she didn't have already. Always best to give plenty of notice she'd said the other day.

She opened all the windows, just a bit so the rain didn't pour in, but it still allowed good ventilation, and then worked her way right through the house. It was so nice to know that everywhere was clean. The floors were hoovered and washed and every surface wiped, the bathroom in particular sparkled. She was very pleased indeed with all the environmentally friendly cleaning products, they not only smelt lovely they also worked really well.

It also made her feel good that she had not harmed anything by using them and they had certainly worked a treat. The whole house smelt clean and looked fantastic.

Well pleased with her efforts she made lunch. She turned the radio on and had just sat down to eat when the happy tune from 'The Archers' announced the start of the program. *'Goodness me, is this program still going after all these years.'* Well it was like she had never stopped listening to it, she was back into the story straight away. It was a bit like having a ready made group of friends and family. She enjoyed listening to the program and thought she might actually like to tune in more often.

In the afternoon she curled up on the sofa with her book, and just enjoyed being warm and snug. She also wrote a couple of letters to good friends. She had so much to tell them about, and then she made a lovely dinner for herself at the end of the day. The rain had poured all day, but she hadn't minded, she had kept busy and felt it had been a good, productive and enjoyable day.

In the evening Lisa rang and they had a long chat, "It sounds absolutely amazing, I simply can't wait to see you."

"Will you be coming up for Easter?" Vera suggested

"I'll have a look and find out how that fits with the off duty, and then I'll let you know- I suppose I'd better book my bed well in advance as you will no doubt be inundated with visitors."

Then she spoke to Ruth as well and she finished with, "I'll see you soon Mum, so I suppose I better get on and get this last little assignment finished."

They rang off, Vera was so looking forward to seeing Ruth and showing her this wonderful place that she now called home.

# 19

**O**ne morning a few days later she decided to go exploring. Whilst having breakfast she buttered a couple of sandwiches. Made a bottle of juice and a flask of tea and put it all in the rucksack. She put on the sturdy well worn walking boots, and looked at the weather out of the window, which looked cloudy but fine at the moment. She packed some rain gear just in case…*'After all this is Scotland'*.

She stopped at the post office first, the list of people interested in beekeeping was getting quite long already, which was great news. It pleased her tremendously that the head mistress had put her name down together with quite a few children.

Vera had an easy recipe for a delicious cake, with honey, spices and ginger pieces, but she better have a trial run, as she had not baked it in an AGA before! She handed Mrs M her shopping list and said that she would return later after her little exploration round the village.

She found the butcher as Jimmy had described. The awning was indeed colourful, and easy to find. The cottages in the village were all small and squat, nestled together, almost providing shelter for each other. The windows were all small, and nearly all of them had pot plants on the windowsills and some also had the most beautiful intricate lace curtains, but only in the bottom half of the window. They hung neatly on thin brass poles. Smoke was slowly emerging from every chimney. It made such a delightful atmosphere and the slight smoke in the air smelt lovely.

The houses all had neat little gardens, which appeared to be the pride and joy of the owners. It looked like there would be plenty of flowers for the bees. The cottages were situated around a large green, a great play area for the children and also good for socialising for the adults. She noticed a few benches, a barbecue area and a circle of stones round a fire pit. All the houses were painted white and all doors and windows were painted blue, the contrast of the colours were eye catching. Vera went into the butcher and introduced herself.

Mr McBurn was a friendly chubby man in his fifties, just beginning to go grey by the temples, with bright red cheeks, small stubby fingers, the most brilliantly blue eyes and a very welcoming smile. He wore a red and white striped apron.

He was a very knowledgeable butcher, and Vera liked him straight away. They had a good chat and he told her a little about the rearing of animals on the island. He was particularly keen on the beef from Drumlanrig Castle in Dumfriesshire. There were a few farmers on the island who reared some highland cattle but there was no abattoir, so the animals had to be ferried over to the market, where they were bought. This meant that most of the meat the butcher sold was frozen and he therefore had quite a selection available. She bought some bacon and some home made sausages.

He told Vera that it was always a good idea to order in advance as she had done the other day, and gave her his business card. He would rather that than disappoint her. She said she was going to explore a little, especially looking at the gardens around that part of the island, and that she would call in for the meat on her way home.

That was no problem at all; he would pack it all up ready for collection. They wished each other a pleasant day.

Vera was particularly interested in the various plants and flowers that would be important for the bees. There had to be early food, like flowering bulbs and hazel, which with its catkins was usually the first pollen provider. There were small gnarled willow trees, with the pretty and important pussy willows, not quite ready yet but the promise was there! There were some spring and summer flowering perennials, bushes and a few fruit trees, and also plenty of ivy, the last pollen provider of the year. These were the plants she was looking for. There were a great variety of various plants and trees, which was encouraging. But they were all small, and gnarled, and all together very windswept. Some of the trees on the outskirts of the village were leaning heavily where the westerly wind had blown unprotected on them for years.

She came past the church and decided to go in. The graves were all well maintained, and the graveyard looked neat and tidy. Here there were many flowers too. The church was bigger inside than she had anticipated. Huge columns held the vaulted ceiling. She recognised the wooden construction from the York Minster, which many years ago had to be replaced after a fire. 'Blue

Peter' the popular children's program set a competition for kids to design the new wooden bosses. She went to sit quietly in the front pew. It was peaceful. The stained glass windows were spectacular. She was definitely going to bring Ruth here.

After a while she came to the end of the little village, and noticed what looked like lots and lots of heather on the hillside. '*That's great*' she thought, '*we can place some of the hives up here out of the way, at least to begin with.*' Heather honey was particularly nice and very sought after.

There were also quite a few stone-walls, providing shelter and quiet corners, so Vera concluded that it all looked very promising. The path out of town was leading to the cliffs and the tea-house.

She walked a fair distance, along the coastal path and found a lovely little sheltered area, where she decided to take a break and enjoy her packed lunch. It didn't take very long before the seagulls had spotted her and started swooping down to see if they would be lucky and she would share! The large screeching birds were very inquisitive and frightening and she quickly finished the sandwiches. As soon as they were gone, so were the seagulls. It was amazing how quickly they had spotted her and how fast they realised that now the food had all gone.

Sitting at this spot and enjoying the peace and quiet in this little sunny corner surrounded by stone-walls, she found that she suddenly felt quite tired. It was sheltered, warm and safe. On closing her eyes; all she could hear was the gentle movement of the sea. She tried to imagine the waves welling up and washing the rocks far below her, and it really did sound as if the sea was breathing. The sun was shining from an almost cloudless blue sky and it was a lovely spring day, one of the first warm ones. Well it was warm out of the wind; the sun still didn't have enough strength to be really warm on its own yet.

It didn't take long before she drifted off, feeling full and completely safe. She snoozed for a while and was slowly surfacing. At first realising the noise of the sea, and opening her eyes she looked at her watch, she must have been sleeping for at least an hour. The sun had moved, and she was now in the shadow. She had better get back, so it would have to be another outing to find the tea house, but that was actually just nice, as she would still have it to look forward to.

On the way home she collected her orders from the butcher and the shop. It was a weighty rucksack, and she quickly got out of breath on the way up to the house. She had to walk a bit slower, and reminded herself that as she was not a spring chicken, it was ok to take it easy.

Back home she started to prepare her dinner. The sausages she had bought looked so delicious and she could hardly wait to taste them. She had some wine left too and she poured herself a glass, to sit and enjoy whilst the meal cooked in the oven. For good measure she had put a baking potato in with the sausages. As she cut a ring around it she remembered the first time she had made baked potatoes. She wanted to impress her student nurse friends. Unfortunately the potatoes exploded in the oven because she didn't know that she had to pierce the skin. What a mess! She only did that once, but goodness me they had laughed at the incident so many times.

Whilst the meal cooked in the oven she wrote her diary, making notes and little drawings of all her observations. Beginning to make her first plans for the bee keeping presentation in her mind. She had decided to make a power point presentation on her computer, which would be the easiest way to get all the information across. She could download pictures and all the various bits of information she would need to make it both interesting and colourful.

It was so easy downloading it all, and she was quite carried away when the timer went to tell her time was up and the meal was ready.

*'Goodness me! I'd forgotten all about the food in the oven! It was lucky I'd put the timer on. Now I know what Mr McBurn ment with a lot of food has been forgotten in an AGA, it was very easy to do.'* She cleared the table, lit the candles, and went to the Aga to check on the meal. When she opened the door the most delicious aroma emerged; with the big gauntlet oven gloves on she pulled out the roasting dish.

"My word this looks good," she exclaimed out loud, and took herself by surprise! *'I think I am going to enjoy cooking in this contraption; it both smells and looks absolutely delicious'.* She served it up on the plate, and put a good dollop of cold butter in the potato, and went to the table. It was dark outside now, and with the light on in the room she could no longer see the jetty nor the buoys. The room was cosy and she enjoyed her meal. She then washed up, tidied the kitchen and another day drew to an end.

## 20

The spring equinox was on the 21st of March, and on the last Sunday of the month they had put the clocks forward. Spring was in the air and now there were spring lambs all over the place. Their little bahh's could be heard everywhere. Potatoes were now chitting in egg boxes on the windowsills. Tomatoes and climbing green beans were growing in containers too, all ready to be planted out when the weather allowed. She had spoken to Jimmy about making some raised beds, which he was very happy to help her with.

She had taken to going for walks as soon as the weather allowed, and she had noticed that many of the wading birds were now sitting on nests. She was careful not to disturb them when she sat with her sketchbook and she had already got many lovely drawings of the nature that surrounded her.

Well aware that tomorrow would be a very busy and exciting day, she decided that she better be one step ahead of herself and have an early night. She was really looking forward to seeing Ruth tomorrow, and to showing her all the new things around her new home. She was wondering how long the survey for the solar panels would take. With all these thoughts buzzing around in her head and the great anticipation for tomorrow, she made her good night tea. Vera got ready for bed with lots of excitement and gratitude for another lovely day in her mind. That evening it took some time before she fell asleep.

Friday morning she woke up with a start. She looked at the alarm clock. It was 8.17 '*Goodness me, I completely forgot to set the alarm last night and the boat arrives at 12 noon, with Ruth and the surveyors*.'

She jumped out of bed and skipped into the bathroom-turned on the water - then half ran out into the kitchen and filled the kettle. She opened the wood burner and threw in a couple of logs onto the dying embers. Then back to the kettle and made a pot of tea. She put the teapot under the tea cosy and went out into the bathroom. She turned the taps off and went back to the kitchen to pour a cup of tea, which she then brought back to the bathroom. She did all this within a few short minutes, galloping around, buzzing with excitement.

Settling in the warm water, she calmed right down, as she realised that in fact she had plenty of time. It would only take about half an hour to walk down to the jetty, and it was only just about 8.30am now. '*So just take a deep breath Vera, there will be plenty of time. What was it you promised yourself? - Absolutely no rushing!* '

She let her body relax and sink down in water once more, letting the water carry her weight. Relaxing deeply, she could feel how her heart rate began to slow down. At breakfast she looked out over the sea, her eyes were eagerly scanning the horizon for the first sign of the ferry. When she finally spotted it her heart leapt with joy, and this time there was a real reason to be excited.

That little dot, which was still so very far away and only just very faintly noticeable, was bringing her daughter. She was so excited that Ruth was coming to see her so quickly; she had in fact been feeling quite guilty about having left the "children" behind on her ego trip. She had told herself on countless occasions that they were old enough to cope without her and that they had their own lives to live. All would be well and she didn't have to worry. But the guilt of leaving them was deep seated and it wasn't easy to convince herself that she had done the right thing. She knew that for her it was perfect, but had she let the kids down?

So now that Ruth wanted to come so quickly was very reassuring, and she really appreciated it. She cleared up the kitchen and made her bed and went over the bathroom, leaving everywhere absolutely spic and span.

She dressed warmly in jeans and a big woollen sweater, and checked the time again and again '*how slowly these hands move when I want them to move fast, once she has arrived I don't mind if time stands still.*' She kept peering out of the window, that little dot was not getting much bigger, only very, very slightly, and goodness me how the time was going slowly this morning.

At eleven o'clock she put on her walking boots and walked down towards the post office. She would watch the ferry come in and see it tie up. All the time she would be watching to see if she could catch an early glimpse of Ruth. She felt sure that Ruth would also be watching out for her and Vera didn't want to disappoint her by not being there waiting on the pier. As she walked down the hill she kept an eye on the ferry, now it was getting noticeably closer and Vera's excitement was almost unbearable.

She called in at the butchers and collected her meat. Mr McBurn was a proper old-fashioned butcher, and had a jolly story for each customer. Apparently he had a phenomenal memory, and would remember many details about his customers. He would remember to ask about someone's cat, and ask how Granny was doing, which made the customers really pleased that he remembered. Later she realised that if you wanted to hear any island news a visit to McBurns would give you plenty of information but it was never malicious gossip. He added up in his head, and when he asked for his money he always said,

"That will be so-and-so much. Exactly!" As he handed her the meat over the glass counter. Afterwards she went into the post office. She was in good time so there was even time for a quick coffee.

"Good morning Vera, you look happy today!" Mrs M greeted her with that well known warm smile. Vera replied that she was indeed happy and so excited too as her daughter was arriving on the ferry. Mrs M said she so understood Vera's excitement and said,

"This is one of the wonderful things about living on the island. Visitors arrive on the ferry with all the anticipation and excitement that brings with it. Are you all ready for your visitor?" Vera confirmed that she was well organised and everything was ready for her first guest.

"To be honest I could hardly fall asleep last night." She sipped the coffee, and told Mrs M that Ruth would be staying a couple of days and that she would like to introduce them to each other, but not today as the solar power people were also coming.

Yes! Mrs M knew that, as they were going to see two more potential customers. "We're one of them! We've taken up your recommendation."

The government had made a good incentive to get the solar panels installations started in the country. Grants were available and also a very good "feed in tariff" it was called. All the kWh generated would be paid at an inflation-protected price for 25 years, whether the customer used them themselves or not. It sounded too good to be true. But the initial pay out for the installation was of course very expensive, but with the long daylight hours in the summer, it would certainly be worthwhile to invest in the scheme Vera thought.

Vera was so pleased to hear that the surveyors were going to see more properties. She had felt guilty about making them travel all the way up here just for her installation survey. Maybe she didn't need to worry about offering them lunch then as they would probably be very short of time as the return ferry would leave again at 3pm.

Several people came into the shop, having a chat and a coffee or a 'wee dram' before going out on the jetty to greet the boat. Vera declined the offer today; she was not going to greet her daughter smelling of alcohol.

## 21

As the ferry was quite close now, she said goodbye and went outside. But it was still not close enough to see any particular person on board, which she realised once she was out on the pier.

Slowly it navigated between the buoys and the cardinal markers, making a safe approach. Callum came out on deck to prepare the mooring warps; the chap who was going to receive them was just arriving on his bike. He greeted people as he walked out on the pier whilst putting on his big leather gauntlets. Vera went out to stand at the very end of the pier, by the small lighthouse with the red glass in the window, eagerly watching out for Ruth. She could see several passengers now, but no

Ruth. This worried her, maybe she had missed the ferry, and maybe she wasn't even coming after all. Whenever Vera had fetched Ruth from the airport or at the train station, she had always been the first one off, so keen to meet again. All sorts of worrying thoughts flew through her mind and she felt her pulse thumping in her throat and her sweater was suddenly too tight around her neck, she tugged at it to let some heat escape from her chest too.

She lifted her hand to her brow to see better and leaned slightly forwards to get an even better look. No! There was still no sign of her. The ferry was quite close now; it was just making the last few adjustments and manoeuvres before Callum would be able to throw the warps ashore. It was fun to watch the mooring from this side, especially now that she knew what was happening. There was that last little blast from the engine to swing the stern in! She remembered it so clearly from her own arrival and the warps were then thrown ashore and fastened expertly with the engine idling. Callum smiled and waved when he spotted her whilst he was securing the gangway.

The ferry had arrived!

And still no sign of Ruth. Vera had been so sure that Ruth would have been out on deck waving, but no- there was no waving Ruth. Maybe she'd missed the ferry! Vera was anxious now as the minutes passed, and there was still no sign of her. She felt her eyes water. She walked towards the gangway.

The passengers were beginning to come ashore, being met and greeted. Vera was bursting with a combination of excitement and anxiety. She stood on tiptoes and craned her neck to be able to see better.

Then she spotted Ruth! and drew a big sigh and felt the shoulders droop. Arrhh what a relief. She felt her shoulders moving back to their normal resting place, she hadn't even been aware how she had tensed them up.

There she was, deep in conversation with a young man. As they approached the gangway they had to go in single file and first then, at last, did Ruth scan the jetty and their eyes met. Vera waved and almost ran the last few steps to greet her with tears of joy in her eyes. They embraced each other, entirely blocking the gangway. The young man Ruth had been talking to was right behind her and he waited patiently whilst mother and daughter hugged.

"Move along please!" said Callum, then nodded and smiled to Vera and gave her a thumbs up. She returned the sign with a smile.

They quickly stepped aside to let others pass. Ruth said,

"Mum, this is Richard, the surveyor you are waiting for. We met on the train." Vera and Richard shook hands.

"Welcome! I suppose you are in quite a rush? I understand you have 3 properties to visit today. So as time is short, let's go quickly."

Ruth was beaming, she looked so happy, dressed in her well-worn blue duffle coat and had a huge multi-coloured scarf and matching knitted hat on. She was carrying her rucksack and had her little leather handbag across her. She always travelled like that.

Vera looked admiringly at her, didn't she just look so well and vibrant. Richard had also got a bag with him with the instruments he would need to do the surveys. The conversation between the three of them flowed easily and the youngsters were full of admiration of the island. The walk to Harbour View seemed to take no time at all.

"What a lovely cottage and what an amazing view" Richard and Ruth were full of praise. Richard had to do some measurements outside of the angles and inclines and size of the roof and used a compass to note exactly the direction of the property. These were all very important parameters for the solar panels installation. If the roof were not in an advantageous direction, the expense of installing solar panels would not be economical. The best situation was facing due south, but the slope of the roof was equally important depending on the latitude of the property. For example a flat roof was completely unsuited up here, but perfect on the equator, Richard had explained on the way. The roof faced south/east on one side of the house, and north/west on the other, not exactly ideal, but Richard expertly calculated how many kWh she would be able to make and it was agreed that she would go ahead.

Richard was able to give Vera a discount too, as she had been kind enough to get him two more surveys to do. This was an unexpected surprise but excellent news for sure.

When all the paper work was done Richard bade them farewell and went on his way. He shook hands with Vera, who went back inside, leaving the youngsters to say goodbye to each other. She heard them say how they had enjoyed meeting, and Richard's final word were:

"I will call you on Tuesday then, and then we can arrange when and where to meet. Ok? Bye for now." And off he went down the track to the next property.

## 22

**W**hilst he had been busy with his measuring outside, Vera had put the kettle on and showed Ruth upstairs, and settled her in. Ruth was most impressed, and Vera was so proud and felt even better about the decision to move north, now that Ruth was so appreciative of it all.

Ruth could se that this was the perfect place for her mother. She already looked about twenty years younger, she was happier than Ruth had seen for a very long time and it was obvious to see that she already felt so much better. Yes, Ruth totally agreed, this had been the right move.

"Well I suppose we ought to think about some lunch" Vera looked at her watch, as Ruth reappeared in the kitchen she had been outside for a little snoop around and it was already quarter past two.

"What do you fancy, Ruth?"

"Well what have you got Mum? You know I'm not fussy." Vera opened the little fridge and peered in,

"I have some quiche Lorraine and…"

"..Your own?" Ruth interrupted

"Yes of course it is! I've even made it in the AGA"

"Well let's have that then, let's warm it first, shall we?" Ruth was enthusiastic, Mums quiches were always delicious, she hadn't realised how hungry she in fact was.

"Let me just place it on a baking tray, then it can warm whilst we lay the table. Vera reached into the cupboard and found a tray to put the fluted dish on. It really did look delicious, and they both commented on how hungry they felt now.

"Poor Richard," Ruth bit her lip. "He never had anything to eat or drink, he was in such a hurry. Well I am sure he can buy something on the ferry when he sails back." Ruth quickly found knives and forks, plates and mugs. She poured milk into a little jug.

Her Grandmother on her father's side had been 'a real lady' with very definite principles; she would never have contemplated putting the milk bottle on the table, nor any other containers for that sake. The butter was always transferred to the butter-dish, and the butter was to be taken from here with the butter-knife, which was not used to butter the bread. Grandmother's horrified face had told the children once and for all that that was not how it was done. The children had always been on their very best behaviour when they visited Grandma; Vera never even had to remind them of manners. At Grandma's excellent behaviour was expected and the children always rose to the occasion.

It was the approving little smirks and winks Grandma made to Vera as the two of them exchanged glances, which went unnoticed by the children who were too busy trying to be well behaved, that made Vera so proud of them.

They reminisced over the childhood memories as the meal became ready to eat. They chatted so easily with each other. Vera quickly made a small salad to have with the quiche. Ruth made the tea, and carried the teapot to the table. With the big oven gloves on Vera opened the AGA when the timer rang, and brought the simmering quiche to the table. Ruth commented on how delicious it smelt and how surprised she was that she had not smelt it cooking. Vera explained about the AGA's special venting system.

Ruth sat so she could see the jetty and the post office, they could see Richard surveying the post office roof, with both Mr and Mrs Morrison looking up and pointing and gesticulating. It was quite fun to watch, especially now that they had an idea of what they might be discussing down there.

"Don't you think he is really nice Mum?" Ruth said looking dreamily out of the window, finding it hard to take her eyes off Richard. "We travelled together on the train, he came and asked if the seat opposite me was taken and sat down. He was just so friendly and easy to talk to; we actually talked all the way up here. It was such a coincidence that we were going to the exact same place. Isn't it really weird? It really makes me think if all this mumbo-jumbo about fate is actually true. Have you ever had an experience like this? I mean, have you met someone that you liked straight away?"

Vera thought for a moment, saying "hmmmm" and frowned. She chewed her mouthful of quiche, slowly and carefully, prolonging the time to give an answer. Her brain was racing, debating with herself whether to tell Ruth about Jimmy now, when the moment had presented itself so beautifully, or to wait.

"MMM-Yeeesss," she was still thinking fast. She decided to be brave and said,

"Yes I have actually, as recently as my first Friday here," she laughed an uneasy almost embarrassed little snigger.

"Oh," Ruth was surprised, "just the day after you arrived? What happened?" Ruth's awareness had immediately returned to the room. "Tell me Mum!" She put down her knife and fork and leant back in the chair. She straightened her napkin on her lap and made eye contact. She was ready to listen.

So Vera told Ruth about Jimmy. She smiled as she talked, just thinking and talking about him made her happy. She told her about the meeting in the post office and of the dance.

She told Ruth about the lighthouse and Sirius and the funny thing about the cakes, and how they had laughed at the coincidence. She also told Ruth that Jimmy was coming for lunch on Sunday. And that Harbour View actually was Jimmy's Grandmother's house, and that his mothers name had been Vera too,

"So I am the second Vera to live here!"

Ruth was all ears! She was well aware of how lonely and sad her Mum had been after her Father had died. She was so pleased for her Mum, she knew that no one could ever take Dad's place in Mums heart, but it was good that she had met a friend that she liked so much.

"Well" she concluded, "It looks like we are both going to have a very interesting spring" she lifted her mug of tea and said, "Here's to happy days! I really can't wait to meet Mr Jimmy. He sounds very special, and he is obviously making you very happy too, this is just great Mum."

Vera smiled; she was so pleased Ruth had accepted the budding friendship so easily.

"This lunch is so delicious Mum, I think you have done really well cooking in this new oven. But let's tuck in before it gets completely cold."

Ruth looked out of the window again and noticed that there was some commotion on the pier, some people were running waving their arms. The ferry had left and was already past the end of the pier. Dark smoke belched out of the chimney, the engine was working hard.

"I wonder what is going on down there? Something is not right." Ruth was looking out of the window. Vera got up and came over to look,

"It looks as if someone has missed the ferry,"

"Goodness me it looks like Richard, Mum." Ruth exclaimed anxiously, getting up from her chair and leaned on the windowsill almost knocking over the sprouting potatoes.

"What shall we do Mum, what is he going to do? Do you think we can help?" Vera grabbed the telephone straight away and rang the post office,

"Hello Mrs M. Vera from Harbour View here. It looks like the surveyor missed the ferry. Would you mind very much to give him a message from me?"

"Nooo, not a-tall." replied Mrs M, in her broad accent.

"Can you see him from the house, is he still on the jetty?" Vera confirmed that and Mrs M said that she would go and find him straight away.

"What's the message?"

"It looks like he has missed the ferry, if you could just ask him to come back up to Harbour View. He is welcome to stay with us for the weekend. Perhaps you would you be kind enough to ring back if he declines the offer? Goodbye and thank you so much for your assistance, he must be quite distraught I can imagine."

"I'm on me whey!" Mrs M hung up.

Looking out of the window they saw several people standing on the pier. The ferry had indeed left and was already out in the open sea.

They saw Mrs M get out of the post office and she must have called them as they all turned as one to face her, and then they walked towards her. They could see she pointed at Harbour View, the little group dispersed and they saw that Richard shook Mrs M's hand and began to walk up the track towards the house.

Ruth and Vera talked about what would be the best solution to this little conundrum. There were two beds in the spare room, Vera had a double bed in her bedroom, and there was also the sofa.

"But he won't have anything for overnight as he has just come for the day, what are we going to do about that?"
They began to clear up after lunch and Vera put the kettle on again.

"Actually, I wonder if he has had any lunch? I think we will leave the table as it is. He will feel more welcome, if we just seat him and feed him, poor thing he must be ravenous. I wonder what plans have been ruined for him by missing the ferry?"

Before Richard reached the front door, the phone went again. It was Mrs M, who said that several people in the Hub had expressed an interest in the solar panels and now the surveyor would be on the island for the weekend. Would it maybe be possible for him to survey some more properties? A few of the crofters that lived further away had come to meet the ferry, and they had only just heard about his visit. Vera said she would ask Richard to return the call, when he arrived.

## 23

Shortly there was a tap on the door, and there he stood, with a sheepish smile, and lifted his hands in an apologetic gesture,

"I'm so terribly sorry to cause such a fuss. What has happened is that I completely forgot to put my watch forward last Sunday, when we changed to summertime. I don't normally wear it, and oh dear this is just so incredibly embarrassing. I really can't thank you enough for your kindness."

"Well you just come inside now, you must be so hungry, come and sit yourself down. We shall soon sort everything out, but before you make yourself too comfortable, would you mind giving Mrs Morrison at the post office a call. She rang before you arrived to say that there were some more people interested in surveys and now you are on the island for the week-end, maybe you would like to consider that."

He bent down in the hallway to take off his big boots, hung his coat on the rail, and went into the living room, where Vera showed him the telephone and dialled the number. Richard told Mrs M. that he would certainly do more surveys and that he would then catch the ferry home on Monday as there was no ferry over the week end, and that should give him plenty of time. He asked if Mrs M. would organise timing, as she would know the different properties and how long it would take him to get from one to the other.

"Please ask people to be a bit flexible as some are quick and others might take a little while, but to give you an idea, it took me 35 minutes to do Harbourview. I am free all of tomorrow, I will keep Sunday free, and then I can do some more again on Monday morning if necessary. I can catch up with any paperwork whilst sailing, this time I shall be at the ferry on time." He laughed a bit embarrassed.

With all that in place he sat down and tucked in to the delicious lunch. The warm tea did him good and restored his soul so to speak and he was so grateful for their hospitality.

"What were your plans for the week-end? I suppose whatever plans you had has now been scuppered?"

"Well, I actually thought with all the travelling during the week, I would need some time to catch up on things at home, so I have actually not got any plans." Richard replied with a shrug of the shoulders.

"Have you by any chance brought an overnight bag with you?"

"No I'm afraid I haven't, I'm terribly sorry to be such a nuisance."

"That is no trouble at all, I will call Jimmy and ask if we may borrow a few bits and pieces from him, I will do that straight away."

She went to the phone, but before she had picked up the handset, it rang,

"Harbour View, Vera speaking."

"Wheel Heelooo therrre!" it was Mrs M, "It's me ageen, I understand you have unexpected guests, are therrre anything yee need, we are harpi to lend the young man anything he needs."

"Arhhhhh! You caught me out, you must be telepathic! You are just so thoughtful. We are actually short of a few things, do you think I could call you back in a few minutes when we've discovered what we'll need, it's mostly over night things I think. I will ring back, and thank you so very much indeed for your thoughtfulness."

So whilst they finished the meal they made a little list of things for the weekend. The two youngsters had no qualms about sharing the two single beds in the spare bedroom. They rang to Mrs M with the list of things. She said she would send her Hamish up in the car with a bag. The youngsters went upstairs to get organised and make up the bed. They were chatting away and appeared completely relaxed in each other's company. It somehow seemed like they had known each other for years. '*Just like Jimmy and I,*' Vera thought to herself as she began to tidy up in the kitchen. Thank goodness she had bought plenty of food. There was plenty of everything.

Richard noticed the log basket was getting empty, and offered to fill it up. He was most impressed with the smart basket on wheels.

The shadows were lengthening as the sun was setting. Ruth lit candles and Vera began to prepare the evening meal.

Richard brought in a brimming basket and put two logs in the fire. He commented on the efficiency of the wood burner and what an amazing amount of heat it was making.

Vera gave Dick, as they discovered he preferred to be called, a bottle of red wine and a corkscrew, and Ruth found some nibbles and glasses. Soon dinner was simmering away in the oven and the three of them sat down with a glass of wine in the comfortable sofa corner.

They heard the car pull up outside, and Vera went to answer the door. Richard brought his wallet, but Mr Morrison wouldn't hear of any payment. He also brought a list of people who would like a survey done the next day. So far there weren't any for Monday, but there were seven for Saturday.

"You'll have a busy day tomorrow I s'pose, and I'm happy to drive you around," he smiled.

Vera asked if Mr Morrison would care to join them in a glass of wine, he laughed and politely declined saying that he didn't drink the stuff, but he

"Wouldn't say nay to a wee dram."

"I'm really sorry, but I don't have any whisky! Will tea do?"

"Don't worry!" Richard saved the situation. "I just bought one in the shop-I couldn't very well come to Scotland and not buy a bottle of whisky could I?"

"Well come on in then," Vera laughed, "You are obviously in luck"

He took off his boots and jacket and he too settled himself in the sofa, Vera and Ruth pulled up a couple of dining chairs. Richard found the whisky bottle, and showed it to Mr Morrison,

"Will this do?" he asked politely.

Hamish laughed heartily,

"Well it's obviously not our local one, as it is actually not for sale, but this is fine, thank you ever so much. Do you think I could have some water with it? A true whisky drinker never drinks whisky neat, you nooh! We always serve whisky with a little jug of water here in Scotland."

Well that was news to Ruth and Dick. Vera had already learnt that the very first day here when she was offered the wee dram in the hub.

"How much water do you put in then?" they wanted to know

"That is completely a personal preference," he answered, lifting the glass and sniffing the golden liquid.

The four of them had a laugh and a good chat, and Mr Morrison stayed for about an hour, before he made his excuses and went back down the hill. He had offered to fetch Dick tomorrow, but Dick said he would like to walk down to the post office. They arranged to meet at nine o'clock and off he went.

The three of them stood in the doorway in the fresh evening air and saw the red lights on the back of the car disappear down the track.

"Brrrrr it ain't half chilly out here, let's get back inside." They all shivered and hurried back inside to the warm cosy room and finished laying the table, and then sat down to a delicious meal.

They finished off with a lovely cup of tea on the sofa in front of the fire sitting there getting drowsy, after such an exciting day.

Dick suggested that the ladies used the bathroom first, whilst he washed up and tidied the kitchen and blew out the candles, and they got ready for bed. Vera explained about the peat turf for the night before she retired. She then said goodnight, and went into her bedroom. As she snuggled down she could hear the soft voices upstairs. She drifted off thinking of how happy and relaxed Ruth was in Dick's company, and what a lovely man he was, strong and reliable, and with big solid hands. 'I know it is early days but I think she might have found Mr Right.'

Vera was remembering the saying that it takes us only seconds to like or dislike a person, and Vera's intuition told her that this was a good relationship. It had certainly had the best start, how lucky he had missed the ferry.

The youngsters carried on talking upstairs long after Vera had fallen asleep. They talked about the good fortune that they had met, and laughed about how Dick had missed the ferry, was that also fate? They smiled at each other across the room and said goodnight.

## 24

Vera was woken by the noise of muffled clattering of crockery, and voices hushed but happily talking; the youngsters were up and in the kitchen already, *'what's the time?* She turned and looked at the alarm clock, 7.11 it said,

"My word they're up early" she whispered to herself. Just then there was a gentle knock on the door.

"Morning Mum, here comes a cup of tea for you" Ruth tiptoed in, in her big ski-socks and placed the cup on the bedside table.

"Thank you ever so much darling, I am awake you know, I heard the two of you in the kitchen just now. Did you sleep well?" Vera pushed herself up in the bed rearranging the pillow behind her. "Look! have you seen the view I have from my bed?" Ruth sat down on the spare side of the bed with a big sigh, and admired the amazing view.

"Oh Mum! I am so thrilled that you have found this lovely place." She turned and smiled at her mum,

"You're really happy here aren't you? It is so obvious to me. You seem so much calmer, you smile a lot and your eyes are brighter, you seem so 'at home'." Vera picked up the cup and sipped the tea, agreeing with a long

"Mmmm, yes it is really strange but I do feel so at home, this feels so right and has done from day one. I don't really know why," she added thoughtfully.

Dick was busy in the kitchen. He obviously felt at home too, and was happy to be useful. He laid the table, boiled the kettle and was just waiting for instructions about what to make for breakfast. The wood-burner was already gently glowing as he had stoked the fire. He was obviously a man who could roll up his sleeves. He was energetic, kind and very enthusiastic. Vera liked him a lot already.

The youngsters were both up washed and dressed, and were just waiting for Vera to get organised; she was surprised that she hadn't woken up when they started rummaging about, they must have been very quiet.

They decided to have a light breakfast of a boiled egg and some toast, and a glass of orange juice. It was already on the table by the time Vera was washed and dressed. Dick buttered himself a sandwich for lunch, and set off for the post-office and his day's work.

"See you later!" he smiled, waving as he went down the trail with strong confident strides. He seemed to walk to a rhythm, they wondered if he might be humming to himself. Unbeknown to the ladies he was actually singing aloud, really loud! As he thought nobody would hear him; his cup was literally overflowing, he was so happy. He felt so right about meeting Ruth; she was the one he had been waiting for:

"Praise Thee oh thy great Jehovah" his voice boomed; he had Welsh ancestors, which would have been easily recognised in that great voice, had anybody been listening.

The sheep looked up from their grazing for a moment, singing was not something they were used to.

The sun was peeping surreptitiously through the clouds, sending golden brushstrokes and strong rays over the pale blue sky, it had all the promises of a nice day ahead.

"What would you like to do today Ruth?"

They were sitting at the breakfast table looking down towards the jetty, the sun was painting the sky pink, yellow and red now, the thick layer of clouds that had made it impossible to determine where the horizon was, were already beginning to disperse.

"Actually, I would quite like to just sit here and talk to you and drink tea. We didn't really get any time yesterday to really catch up, and we also need to prepare the meal for tomorrow, and I am sure there are things I can help you with in general, aren't there?"

Vera smiled; Ruth was her usual helpful and considerate self.

"Yes Darling, let's just sit and talk and see how the day goes, there aren't really any jobs that needs doing as such, but I would like you opinion at some point on where and how you think the kitchen garden should be situated and designed."

"That is a great project Mum, have you thought about what you would like to grow?"

They sat at the table for a long time and had a really good chat.

The solid foundation for their relationship had been laid years ago, when Ruth was a tiny baby. Vera had treated her like she would have treated her very best friend. She had always been attentive to the baby's needs and listened to her whatever she was communicating, from the minute she was born. She was never left to cry, and had always been made to feel valuable and important. It had given Ruth a deep inner strength and a self-confidence that had enabled her to reach out and be there for others at a very early age. She was now studying to become a Vet, and Vera knew that she would be excellent at her job. Not just looking brilliantly after the animals and not just because she was clever and could absorb the copious amounts of knowledge necessary, but especially because of her very well developed compassion and empathy, which made her so well suited to look after the owners too.

Martin had thought that she would make an excellent doctor, and she certainly would, but Vera's reason to push for the Vet studies rather than medicine had been because she feared medicine would drain Ruth emotionally and burn her out fast. She would not have been able to leave the patients and go home, and if she did, she would have had to ring in and find out how Mrs So-and-So was doing, and she would have been distraught if a patient died under her care. Being a vet, it was still hard to lose a patient, but they were after all animals, not someone's mother, husband or even child.

Ruth was very happy in her studies, and had only another year to do once the exams in June were over. This next year would be mainly practice and hands-on, both operating in the veterinary hospital and consulting in the general veterinary practice at the school. Ruth was enthusiastically telling Vera all about exciting operations, especially on exotic animals that had come in from a Zoo, with very exciting problems. It was really fascinating and all in a day's work.

She was very keen on large farm animals and would have preferred to work with them, but she was not so keen on the farmers general attitude, as they often just shot an ill animal rather than spending money on the vet.

The small animal practices were on the other hand fun and very varied; you never knew what would come through the door. It could be a child with a hamster, a dog owner, or a lonely old boy with his canary; you had to use all your people skills as well as your vast education.

Ruth often thought doctors were lucky, they only had one body to learn about, she had to learn about mammals, reptiles, birds and fish, and as people got hold of more and more exotic pets like tarantulas and chameleons, not to mention snakes, the knowledge she had to have at the ready was almost a bottomless pit.

They cleared up the breakfast, aired the house, tidied up everywhere, and prepared the food for tomorrow's lunch and tonight's dinner, whilst they chatted. Then they went out into the garden and had a look at where Vera could place the kitchen garden she was quite sure she wanted raised beds, maybe built in a rectangle.

It was a lovely mild morning. The sun was out now, and they decided to bring out the deck chairs and sit and look for a little while, smell the smells and hear the noises.

Vera reminded Ruth of what old Grannie Farm used to say, 'sometimes I sit and think, and sometimes I just sit'.

"Such wise words Mum! And how seldom do we allow ourselves to actually do precisely that, just sit. We are always busy, we have to be industrious and we could certainly not be seen to be lazy could we."

But today they could just sit. They didn't have to talk all the time, they were happy to share silence too. After a while Ruth fetched her sketchbook and started making notes, just as Vera had imagined she would.

She closed her eyes, she really could not be happier.

When she opened them again, she realised she must have nodded off as Ruth had finished a sketching of the kitchen garden, complete with a beehive and a chicken coop. It looked absolutely fantastic, and Vera was thrilled. She had designed the raised beds, and there was room for just about all the things Vera wanted to grow. She had even included a meadow area for wild flowers for the bees. Whether it would be possible in Scotland, that she would have to ask Jimmy about, after all he had lots of years of experience having had to be self-sufficient at the lighthouse for years. Vera suggested they showed him when he called in for lunch tomorrow.

Suddenly they heard a knock on the door. Jimmy was just on his way back home from the usual Saturday trip to the post office. He had of course brought good old Sirius, who was glad of some fresh water, and a rest! The three of them sat on the sofa and enjoyed a little half an hours chat and a cup of tea. Ruth and Jimmy hit it off straight away, they had the same dry sense of humour. It would be nice to spend longer tomorrow for lunch, they all agreed. Jimmy and Sirius was soon on their feet heading back home to the lighthouse-

"See you tomorrow then and thanks for the tea."

After lunch Vera asked,

"Would you perhaps like to meet my neighbours, Karl and Emma, and their little boy Simon? They live just a little walk round that headland over there." She pointed with her right thumb over her shoulder. Ruth thought that would be great and they put on their walking boots and weather proofs, and off they went.

The track went along the lee shore where they could see sheep munching on the seaweed;

"I had no idea they would eat anything but grass, you wait until I tell my mates about this, they will be so surprised." There were lots of wading birds too with long legs and curved beaks busy picking out a meal along the shore and of course the oystercatchers with their strong red beaks. The waves were gently lapping along the shore with a long lazy swishhhh as they went in and out of the sandy cove.

There was that distinct smell of washed up drying seaweed, and the birds were busy chasing the creepy-crawlies living in it. It was all very peaceful and harmonious. Ruth noticed how quiet it was and commented on it.

They rounded the headland and saw the neighbours working in the garden. Simon spotted them first, "Harloooo Vera!" he shouted and waved and ran towards them and threw himself at her with a biiig hug. That got the parents attention and they went toward them and greeted them smiling.

"Hi there my darling boy! " She squatted down and hugged him. "This is my daughter Ruth Simon, she is visiting for the first time, and I thought it would be nice if you met each other, then you both know who I am talking about!" The adults exchanged handshakes.

"So you are already busy in the garden" Ruth said looking around.

"Yes" Emma pointed, "look the spring bulbs are beginning to surface, and it is such a lovely mild day, we thought we'd get out and have a little rummage and get some fresh air and make the most of it. The weather has been unusually kind since your Mother arrived Ruth, we're not used to such a lot of sun so early in the year, but long may it last Vera."

"Yes hopefully it won't be long before we can get started in the gardens in earnest. When spring arrives, there will be enough to do to keep us busy, so it is good to get a head start." Karl added.

"Well we won't hold you up, we were just out to familiarise Ruth with my fantastic surroundings, so we will be off again" they bade each other farewell and went back the way they had come, everything was looking different now that they were facing the opposite direction. From here they could see the bay and the post office and the village, Vera could point out various places, and soon they were back at the cottage again.

"Let's put the kettle back on shall we?"

"Definitely!" Ruth was more than ready for a piece of mums home made cake, and tea could as far as she was concerned, be drunk morning noon and night, and in copious amounts.

As they munched the cake and tea they began to talk about the evening meal and discussed what preparations needed to be done?

## 25

The dinner was going to be fish pie. Vera had found the recipe from the first evening meal in the Village Hall on the internet, as that Jamie Oliver fish pie had been so amazing at the ceilidh! As it had been so delicious she had decided to make it for Ruth, they talked about how they hoped that Dick liked fish too.

"Well if we are unlucky and he hates fish we will find him something else but not to worry, we will cross that bridge when we get to it." Vera said reassuringly.
The afternoon had gone so quickly, the sun was already low in the sky,

"Is the sun over the yardarm yet?" Vera gave Ruth a wink," would you like a glass of wine as we cook?" she looked over at Ruth who nodded smiling,

"White please Mum," she said without lifting her head from the chopping board. She was getting the vegetables ready.

There was a knock at the door and the sound of the latch, and big boots in the hall.

"Hello-oh!" Sounded a happy voice; it was Dick returning. He left his coat and boots in the hall, and came into the living room. He went straight to Ruth and gave her a massive hug;

"I have had the most amazing day, I have met such nice people, and I have some orders in my book, I really can't believe what a fantastic experience it has been to come here."

He went to Vera and took her in his arms too,

"It is all thanks to you Vera, I am so grateful!"

"Well don't mention it, would you like a glass of wine? As you can see we have already started."

"Let me just go and wash my face, then I will join you." He scanned the worktop,

"I will join Ruth in the white I think, see you in a minute."

They could hear him rummaging about first upstairs, and then in the bathroom. Soon he appeared freshened up, teeth brushed, smelling of soap and with nice red cheeks from being outside all day.

"Can I help" he joined them at the worktop, "Cheers!" he lifted his glass, and without thinking about it, gave Ruth a peck on the cheek, as the most natural thing in the world. She smiled and leaned into him, raised her glass, and looked into his eyes,

"I am so very glad I met you Dick, cheers" they touched the glasses and Vera joined in,

"Here is to many happy get-together's at Harbour View!! Cheers both of you." They all touched glasses.

"Dinner will soon be ready, would you like to lay the table Richard?"

They had a lovely evening together, and before going to bed Vera put the prepared lamb shoulder in the roasting oven for twenty minutes to seal it and then placed it in the simmering oven, just like Butcher McBurn had advised. She was not familiar with this 'slow-cooking overnight' business and was quite looking forward to tasting the result the next day.

She let the youngsters settle first. As she pottered about in the kitchen she could hear their muffled conversation upstairs. They suited each other perfectly, she thought. She made her mug of tea and went to the bathroom, and finally snuggled into bed. Tomorrow she would be seeing Jimmy again; she felt the corners in her mouth curl into a smile. Yes! Life was good here, there was no doubt about it.

## 26

Sunday morning! And today Jimmy would be coming over with Sirius. She'd woken early and with that happy feeling inside of an exciting day ahead. It was only 06.50, so she got up really quietly so as not to wake the youngsters. It was a fresh chilly morning; it had been a starry night, with no cloud duvet to keep the world warm the temperature had dropped. The thermometer said 2 degrees C, it didn't look as if there had been a frost. She filled the kettle and the wood-burner. Again she was amazed at the peat turfs; they really did smoulder well, and soon she had a cheery fire going again.

She sat for a little while just watching the fire, drinking her tea. She was really looking forward to seeing Jimmy today.

Suddenly she remembered the dinner and rushed to the oven to check the meat. She had forgotten all about it, and of course there had been no aroma in the kitchen to give the game away. *'Note to self Vera, don't forget what has been put in the oven!'*

She opened the simmering oven and lifted the roasting tin out. This was the most delicious looking piece of lamb you could ever wish to put your teeth into. The meat nearly fell off the bone.

She took a deep sniff ummm! It smelt better than she had ever smelt another piece of lamb. She covered it again and put it back in, and closed the door. The only thing she was not so keen on with this oven was that it was at floor level so she had to crouch right down to get to it. But the cooking over night had obviously worked extremely well.

She went back to the sofa with her tea. What else would she need to do before Jimmy arrived? She made one of her lists; peel potatoes, make the yorkshire pudding mixture,( p.s. find the cooking book!) Even though she had made yorkshire puddings for years she had always had to look up the recipe. Vegetables were to be prepared too; she had potatoes, sprouts, carrots and parsnips and of course the pudding. But first they should have some breakfast.

She would hop in the bath, and get ready, then the youngsters could sleep a little longer. She ran the bath, and was just shampooing her hair when she heard the front door open and there was a rustling of boots and coats and hushed voices.

Blow me down if the youngsters hadn't sneaked out for a morning walk before she was even awake, and she hadn't heard a thing. She mused to herself how she had been ever so quiet in order not to disturb them, and then they were already out and about. This bode well for the future she thought, it was good for a young couple to have a good portion of both "get up and go" and zest for life.

She called out a cheery "Good morning!" and Ruth answered back

"Morning Mum, we thought you were up when we saw the smoke from the chimney, have you had tea?"

"Yes! And there is more in the pot, I'll be out in a few minutes"

"No worries Mum, just take your time, we'll get breakfast ready."

She rinsed the hair with the shower attachment, and leaned back into the amber coloured water and felt her body float. Well not exactly float, but certainly being buoyed, and wondered why it is that we all enjoy a bath so much.

She wouldn't have time for the Sunday service today, but that didn't matter, she had company and that was much more important. She got dressed and opened the bedroom windows, flipped the duvet back over the end of the bed so it could air, and closed the door to the bedroom and went into the living room.

"Morning!" She greeted the youngsters who looked so fresh and rosy cheeked after their walk.

"Where did you walk to?"

"We went down through the village and out on the other side to the cliffs. The waves were crashing on the rocks like thunder, and we talked about how powerful the water was. If this was the force on a reasonably quiet day, then what must it not be like in a storm. It's got to be spectacular. We also wondered about how this phenomenal energy could be harnessed, and put into good use."

Richard had shown Ruth some of the properties that had ordered the solar panels, and explained how these installations were going to make a big difference to the island's energy consumption. He had been very impressed with the islander's keen interest in being environmentally friendly. They had come to the conclusion during the walk that if you lived in such close proximity to the environment you were probably much more aware of the importance of your own actions and their influences on your surroundings. Living in a town where sewage just disappeared down the drain, literally! You had no idea of where it went or the impact on the environment. Same with rubbish, we put it in a bin, the bin gets emptied, but what happens to it after that most of us are ignorant about.

"When do you think Jimmy will arrive?" Ruth poured the tea.

"Probably for coffee at about eleven, at least that is what I have invited him for. He will be walking over with Sirius, and it takes about 45 minutes, so yeah, about eleven I should think there will be a knock on the door. I have made a small list of what needs to be done before then."

Ruth smiled and sent a wink to Dick, "You and your lists Mum."

They had a look through it and decided who did what so it would all be ready for when Jimmy arrived.

Vera went to the bathroom, brushed her teeth and put a comb through her hair, perhaps a little squirt of perfume? She looked in the mirror, lipstick? No better not, that would make it much too obvious that she was excited to see him, and now she regretted the perfume and washed it off with a flannel. She felt it was important that she was herself, just herself, no fuss and bother. But at the same time she realised that she was *really* looking forward to seeing him again.

She went back into the living room after having tidied the bedroom and closed the windows again. Everything was ready, table laid for coffee, vegetables prepared, the Yorkshire pudding mix was in the fridge, even the gravy was made. Everything was ready for a really nice day ahead.

"Are you nervous Mum?" Ruth asked and came up to Vera and put her hands on her shoulders and looked into her eyes.

"Nooohh!" She looked away, avoiding Ruth's inquisitive eyes, a little shy.

"Well, yes! Perhaps a bit, it is a rather big thing introducing a new friend, I so hope you will like each other."

"Of course we will Mum, *You* like him! And if you like him I am very sure we will too, I liked him yesterday and

I am just looking forward to getting to know him better." Ruth was very reassuring and embraced her mum warmly.

There was a knock at the door, Vera took a last glance round the room, yes everything was in order, she smiled at Ruth who winked back, and then she went to let the visitors in.

## 27

They'd had a good walk, Sirius was getting older and was not so bouncy anymore, he had been happy to just walk next to Jimmy.

Jimmy always walked with a long stick; it was well worn at the bottom and where his thumb rested in the fork. His face was rosy, and as he bent over and hugged Vera, she could smell the fresh air and clean soap on his cheek. The tickling softness of his beard on her cheek was just so lovely.

He took off his wax jacket, and boots, found his slippers in the pocket and made Sirius lie down in the hall on the small blanket he'd brought in his rucksack.

"Does he have to stay out here? Vera asked."He is welcome in the living room where we are. He seemed so happy by the wood burner before."

"Well if you are sure you don't mind, then we will just move his blanket, where will he be least in the way?"

"You know him best Jimmy, just put it where he will be happy. Shall I put a bowl of water out for him?"

"Vera you seem to think of everything, yes please that would be very nice." Jimmy was not accustomed to fuss like this.

They went into the living room and Vera introduced Dick and Jimmy to each other.

"What a lovely smell of real coffee" Jimmy breathed deeply in through his nose. "It's not often you get this anymore, since the powder coffee has been invented. It takes me right back to years ago."

"Yes! Let's sit down and have a cup of coffee" Vera said smiling and they gathered round the little table. Once they had sat down Sirius got up from the blanket and went to the water-bowl. He was thirsty, he slopped and slurped and nearly drank it all, and then as a good boy he went round and round three times and lay down on the blanket put down for him, and went to sleep with a contented hrmph.

The conversation round the table flowed easily. They were all intrigued by the new friendships, so lots of questions were asked, as everyone was keen to learn more about each other.

There was plenty to talk about: solar panels, lighthouse life, work as a vet, the island life on the whole, kitchen gardening and beekeeping, there was never a dull moment.

At last it was time to make the last preparations for the dinner. Vera took the lamb out of the oven, Jimmy came and looked over her shoulder, "Wow Vera doesn't that just look good and it smells delicious."

She smiled back over her shoulder meeting his eyes,

"Well for a first timer with the AGA I haven't done too badly I don't think."

Jimmy nodded approvingly he was well used to an Aga, and wouldn't be without his for love nor money. He said,

"It's like a friend really."

When everything was ready they served up and Dick poured them all a glass of red wine. Then they sat down for a delicious Sunday lunch, even the Yorkshire puddings were a success. It had always been a family joke about Yorkshire puddings. When Vera made Yorkshires for the family they turned out lovely, but if they had visitors they became either flat like pancakes or if they did rise beautifully they'd be stuck to the tin. So before opening the oven they used to say: "Friends or family?" and today it was definitely FAMILY. They had risen beautifully and popped out of the tin like nobody's business.

Vera felt better today than she had for years, having a table full of jovial people was just so enjoyable, Ruth caught her eye and winked.

"Cheers everybody" she lifted her glass, "and here's to many, many more happy Sunday lunches at Harbour View. I am going to send you a visitors book Mum so you can keep records of who visits and when. Thank you for having us and for this delicious meal. I am actually glad you are going to live all the way up here Mum, otherwise we run the risk of becoming the size of a house with lovely food cooked like this. So you just watch out Jimmy, and keep and eye on that waistline!"

"Yes with dinners like this and your mum's famous cakes and flapjacks, I haven't got a hope of staying slim." He joked.

She laughed and smiled warmly at him. He raised his glass to Vera,

"Here's to a super lady who I have had the good fortune to meet, thank you Vera. Thank you for asking us over for dinner and for introducing me to this lovely couple."

Dick and Ruth looked at each other and smiled, - couple? He reached over the table and took her hand,

"Well we are aren't we?"

Jimmy looked worried at Vera, he grimaced, pulling his mouth wide and lifted his eyebrows questioning.

"Oopsy-daisy, how clumsy of me," He quickly apologised.

Ruth noticed immediately that he was feeling uncomfortable, and before Vera could explain, Ruth quickly butted in with,

"We only met on Friday on the train coming up here."

"I am really sorry, I just assumed!" Jimmy blushed embarrassed.

"No worries." Dick was quick. "It gave me an opportunity to nail it, and yes it all points in the direction that we are a couple, or let me put it like this, we certainly have a super foundation to become one, don't we? So here's to us Ruth!" He ventured and raised his glass and they all toasted again.

They sat at the table for a long time as the conversation flowed so easily. They had dessert and coffee and at the end helped each other with the washing up. It had been a really lovely and very interesting afternoon and time had flown by. At nearly half past five Jimmy decided that he'd better be on his way home again before the light went.

There were big warm hugs all round, everyone thanked one another for a lovely afternoon. Sirius got up from the blanket; he understood it was time to go. He stretched and yawned; he'd had a lovely long snooze, but could do with getting out again now.

As soon as Jimmy and the dog had rounded the headland and were out of sight, the others flopped on the sofa, with another glass of wine reminiscing over the weekend and what a fantastic time they'd had. What a lovely place this island was, and what a thoroughly nice and genuine man Jimmy was.

Tomorrow their journey went back home again, and Vera asked of the youngsters' plans for the week. Dick was particularly keen to get back to his office with the order book. This had been his best ever day of surveys and he thought there was a good possibility that there might be a bonus in the pipeline. Maybe even a promotion.

Ruth returned to clinics every day, and she had to get serious now about revising for the big exam in June. So from that point of view it was not exactly the best time to start a new relationship, as spare time would be rather limited.

They made a cold meat sandwich and a cup of tea later, and sat and chatted until about ten o'clock, when they reluctantly decided to turn in for the night, there was a busy day ahead of them all tomorrow.

When Vera finally made it to bed with her cup of tea, she was tired but happier than she had been for a very long time, but at the same time she did not look forward to the goodbye tomorrow.

## 28

Monday morning came too fast! It seemed like no time at all since she went to meet the ferry on Friday lunch time. And soon it would be time to send the youngsters off on the ferry. She cleaned up in the kitchen after breakfast and stripped her bed, whilst the bedroom was being aired; being such a nice sunny day she thought she would strip the beds and wash the bed linen, and stick to her old monday routine.

She got the youngsters packed up and together they walked down to the ferry. Dick and Ruth walked hand in hand, he with his briefcase, she with her rucksack. They went by the post office to say goodbye and see you again, to Mr Morrison and Mrs M.

Dick also thanked them for sorting him out for the weekend and said that he would be in touch very shortly about the solar panels.

Then it was time to board the ferry, they said a cheery goodbye, as they all knew that they would be seeing each other again before too long.

Vera sent a very happy couple off, and stood on the pier until she couldn't see them anymore. Then she went into the HUB and ordered a coffee and a 'wee dram' and a lovely piece of cake. She watched the little red ferry as it sailed away with its precious cargo.

As she walked back home she went over the weekend-hadn't it just flown by! And yet it seemed like ages ago that she was sitting with Ruth drinking tea in the garden, and she had sketched her plan for the vegetable patch. It made Vera smile when she remembered that Ruth had included a beehive and a chicken coop. And meeting Dick - what a genuinely nice fellow he was.

She was going to miss their company for sure. When she got home the washing machine had finished and she got it all on the line. What a great sight to see it all blowing in the wind. She went upstairs, and found a note on the beds, one from each of them to thank her for the fantastic weekend. She looked out of the window, and she could just see the ferry in the far distance.

She had a small twinge of sadness, but decided to think of the good time they'd had instead of the sadness that they had left. She went back downstairs and made herself some lunch. A nice cold meat sandwich and a cup of tea, she brought it outside, to sit in the sun, where she could sit and watch the linen blowing on the washing line-such a delightful sight. She made notes from the youngsters visit, trying to remember everything that had happened, it had been such an eventful weekend.

# 29

At lunchtime one day Mr Morrison rang to say that some beekeeping equipment had arrived, and would Vera like him to bring it all up to her.

"Oh yes please! That would be great! How many boxes are there?" Where was she going to store them? "What sort of time have you got in mind?" She had rather hoped to catch a little afternoon nap, as she had been awake a lot in the night as the fog horn at the lighthouse had been blowing on and off. It was a very loud and deeply penetrating haunting noise that made everything vibrate. It rattled the cutlery in the drawer and made the glasses tinkle on the shelf.

Mr Morrison called in the late morning, and Vera helped him carry the seven boxes up from the car. Mr Morrison stayed for a cup of tea and a chat.

He commented on what a pleasant young man Richard had been, and together they agreed how exciting it was going to be to get the solar panels installed. Vera also asked if he had heard the noise from the foghorn in the night, and had it kept them awake too?

"We get an awful lot of fog here, and then the shipping can't see the lighthouse, so the fog horn is very important." He reassured her that she would get used to it, and that he just thought about how the noise kept the sailors safe, if he did hear it.

Great was her excitement unpacking and checking everything. Finally all her old gear had arrived, she would have to unpack it all and see what she had and if anything needed replacing. Several new boxes had arrived from Thornes too; it was great they'd arrived together, old and new.

She thought she would bring the wood for making frames and the wax foundation to the bee-keeping afternoon, then everybody could have a go at making frames for the hives. Frame making is a nice but time consuming job, and this way many hands would make light work.

There were several boxes, and Vera and Mr Morrison had quite a job stacking them all in her little entrance hall. All she had ordered was there, and there was even a letter too, that said if anybody did decide to become beekeepers after the presentation, Thornes of Wragby would be happy to give a 10% discount.

'*Wow! What a great offer*', Vera thought, hopefully she could inspire a few people to take up beekeeping. They wouldn't need many hives to get some honey production going.

She was full of enthusiasm, and once Mr Morrison had carried on with his tour of deliveries, she sat down to start making her power-point presentation on the computer. It flowed easily once she got started, and by the end of the afternoon she had finished a really colourful, interesting and very informative talk.

She had called the talk: "Life in a beehive" and had described how the queen can lay up to 2500 eggs a day in the prepared cells that the worker bees build on the wax foundation sheets the beekeeper places in the frames in the hive. She explained how the little creatures grow and develop from a tiny egg, to a larva to a bee, in their short, only 35 day long, lives in the summer. Winter bees live longer.

These cells can also be used to store honey and are so cleverly constructed that they tilt inwards at 20 degrees, to keep the honey from running out. The nectar is passed from the forager to a house bee, she passes it to another and another and once the nectar has been through enough honey stomachs and has become honey because of the enzymes working on it. It is then stored until enough water has evaporated and it has the right water content. Then the cell will be capped with a thin layer of wax.

There were lovely colourful pictures of good plants for bees, pictures of apiaries, and of clothing and tools, and at the end some products made from the hives. Honey of course, which could have various colours depending on where and on what the bees had foraged, wax candles, furniture polish, hand cream just to name a few, and if anyone was interested mead could be made too. Not quite as good as whisky though, Vera smiled to herself, as she imagined how mead would be greeted by the islanders.

Job well done, she said to herself, as she packed it all away, she was quite sure this would spur someone into becoming a beekeeper. Then all there was left to do was to pack up some clothing, the hive tools, the smoker, the veil and make some food with honey in it. Flapjacks and cakes were always a winner, as samples for people to taste, and the afternoon would be complete.

She felt very excited about it and wasn't the least bit nervous now all the preparation was done. *'All we need now are the bees'* she smiled to herself.

The beekeeping afternoon on Saturday was a great success. Twenty-three people turned up, and took a great interest in all the equipment Vera had laid out on the tables. It was important that they could feel and smell it all. They could see the brittle propolis on the old super. This is made from plant sap and is a sticky substance which stains everything bright yellow and becomes brittle with time and the bees use it to secure and glue the hive together, plug holes and generally smoothe everything out.

There was great interest in the subject of bee keeping and everybody understood the importance of keeping bees, and why we must look after them properly. Einstein apparently said that once the bees die we won't survive very long as they are so important for pollination.

That we are able to take their honey and make candles from their wax is just pure bonus. Eight people were interested to learn more and in due course become beekeepers. So it was decided that Vera would hold beekeeping days all the way through the summer as the hives should be inspected approximately every ten days, so they could all learn this ancient skill hands on. Vera would provide the teaching but every one would have to bring their own clothes. She contacted Thornes and got the promised discount for the little group of beekeepers in the making who would now meet on a Wednesday evening weather permitting, once the bees had arrived.

## 30

A few days later Jimmy called in on his way past, they had a cup of tea and a chat. He had really enjoyed the bee keeping afternoon the other Saturday and was really spurred on. He would go back to the lighthouse, as he was sure there was some old stuff in one of the out houses. Adam had enjoyed keeping bees. He rang back later, he had indeed gone to check it out, and he said,

"You are not going to believe it Vera, but there were actually some bees in there, they weren't flying around, they are just quietly walking about on some old boxes, I think they live in there, but I didn't dare fiddle about with them...do you think you could come over and have a look with your veil and gloves on?"

"Sure! I'll come over, it won't be long before they will start flying and it would be great if we could get them into a beehive before the season starts in earnest"

They arranged that she should come over for lunch the following day, as Jimmy had said, that he would really like her to come sooner rather than later, so that was arranged and they rang off.

Vera went to pack all she needed so she could set off the next morning, she was really looking forward to seeing what she might find. She packed an extra veil and gloves for Jimmy, they were her son Michael's old ones, he used to come and help lift and carry when Martin got poorly and couldn't help anymore. She expected there might be a bit of lifting required and in that case better him than her! That old slipped disc didn't bother her that much now, but better safe than sorry. She rang Mr Morrison and asked whether he would be able to give her a lift and also to bring a hive in the car. He reassured her that that would be no problem at all.

How nice it would be to be doing a job together, she was quite excited by the prospect of spending the day with Jimmy.

She went to find the wood and foundation to make frames, the hammer and the little jam jar with the red lid, which contained the little black tacks, and brought it all into the dining table. She put a chopping board down to protect the table and started making frames. The smell of the pine wood and the wax foundations soon filled the room with aromatic scents. As the shadows began to lengthen and another lovely day drew to an end, she finished the frames and tidied it all up, packed and ready for tomorrow.

She made eleven rectangular wooden frames, it didn't take long in her skilled hands. She had no idea what sort of brood chambers there were at the lighthouse or if her frames would fit, but if they didn't she could always ask Mr Morrison if he could drop one of her commercial brood chambers over to Jimmy. She had commercial brood chambers and national supers that worked well for her. Most of her equipment was made of pine, even though cedar wood was recommended, it was just cheaper to use the pine. She had never been made of money, and certainly only had a very limited amount to spend on her bee-keeping hobby.

It had helped that she had been able to sell some honey to friends and family, and occasionally the little corner shop had taken a few jars. She had also been able to sell a few to people with asthma and hay fever.

They usually came and knocked on the door and asked if there was any honey for sale when they felt bad. She had never had to advertise, people just found her when they needed her honey and she had been pleased to help them.

Her thoughts had wandered, as she timbered with the frames, back to London to the little sunny back garden, overlooked by neighbours, there were always noises around her. Either dogs were barking, babies crying, children playing, people arguing, or music was blaring, '*it was never peaceful like it is here, all I hear here are nature noises, the waves, the wind, the crowing cockerel in the morning.*' That was of course apart from the foghorn that she had already acquainted herself with. Again she realised the warm homely feeling this island was already giving her, she definitely felt so at home here, it was almost uncanny.

The next morning she got up and got her chores seen to as a priority, and then set off for the lighthouse with Mr Morrison. It was overcast and no doubt looked like rain, which was a blessing really, as the bees would certainly not be flying if it rained. Jimmy was pleased to see her, Mr Morrison helped to unload and then he was on his way again.

"Shall we go and have a little peep before we eat? He suggested. Vera thought that would be a great idea, then she could see what she needed to get ready, equipment wise.

They had a quick cup of tea, whilst Vera explained what she was hoping to do: First they had to identify where the bees lived, then estimate how big the colony was. It could be enormous if it had lived sheltered and un-disturbed in the shed for years. She needed to see if she could find the queen, because if she could get hold of HER, the rest of the colony would follow, so that was indeed a priority. It was also important not to disturb the colony more than absolutely necessary, so a calm and methodical approach was the order of the day.

"Are you worried about them buzzing around you?" She asked, and as he shook his head she continued, "have you ever had an allergic reaction to bee or wasp stings?" Jimmy could not recall ever being stung, so he didn't think it would be a problem. They finished the tea and gathered all the gear,

"Do you have some matches?" Vera asked, "I forgot to pack some."

When Jimmy came back to Vera with them, she had already put on her white overall and wellington boots, and she had put Jimmy's veil and gloves to one side. Together they went down to the sheds. It had just started to spit and they were glad to get inside. Jimmy showed her where he had found the bees yesterday, but now there was not a sign of them.

"How strange! I swear I saw them yesterday, just over there on those two boxes, they just walked in and out of the little gap there, you see, just over there," he pointed to a small gap between two boxes, the problem was that there were not just two boxes in this shed, there were at least twenty stacked up surrounding where he said he had seen the bees.

"Don't worry Jimmy, they have gone back to the colony because of the rain. We shall just have to move some of the boxes so we can get to them. Here if you take them away as I get them down, she had found a box to stand on so she could reach better. She started from the top on the right hand side. Apart from dust it was empty. But behind it a big spider was disturbed and hastily hid. Vera shuddered; spiders were definitely not one of her favourites. Jimmy noticed and asked if she was ok.

"Yes I am fine, I just disturbed a rather large spider. I can manage mice, but not spiders. Especially not the big hairy ones, and this one was really big."

The second box just underneath was empty too. She moved towards where Jimmy had seen the bees, but more slowly now she knew there were spiders about. She had started at the top, as bees like to work their way down if they are building wild comb, and just because they appeared to get into the colony at their waist level, didn't necessarily mean that that was where the colony was.

When she got to the fourth row in, she made a few puffs with the smoker and then she could hear the buzz. Which was the first alarm call to the colony: Watch out! There is fire about!

She climbed down from the boxes and whilst waiting she told Jimmy that the bees would now go to their honey stores and gorge themselves, in case they would have to leave. The buzz calmed down again; obviously it had been a false alarm. All the bees could return to what they were doing, but now even more quietly as they all had a belly full of honey.

She proceeded even more carefully now. She removed the box that had caused the stir, very, very carefully and yes there they were. It was not a huge colony. She estimated that they would most likely fit into one brood chamber, but if she was lucky and they had made queen cells, she would be able to put those honeycombs in a nucleus box. And if that was the case, she could be lucky and come away with two colonies.

There were five sheets of wild comb in all, she broke it off from the outside. The outside comb on both sides contained honey and pollen and there were not that many bees on them. The honey stores she removed gently with her hive-tool, and put the comb into a big bucket. But as she got nearer to the cluster, where she presumed the queen was, the bees got more and more agitated. *She* wasn't worried, but Jimmy was not really too enthusiastic, he had never had so many bees around him. Vera had explained the importance of being quiet and not to start flapping around. She had told him if he got worried just to walk quietly away.

She placed the brood sheets in the brood chamber, into which she had already placed a few frames with foundation. She managed to get the whole cluster comb into the brood-chamber. She put the lid on, and proudly turned to speak to Jimmy, who was suddenly nowhere to be seen. She left the brood chamber now it was safe to do so and all there was left was just to wait for the rest of the bees to fly in and join the queen. She closed the door to the shed and went to look for Jimmy. He was sitting outside, leaning against the shed wall,

"Hey what's up?" She bent down and looked at him. His eyes were swollen, and he was having trouble breathing.

"Did you get stung?" This could be very serious, he nodded.

"Where did you get stung? Have you removed the sting?"

"I got stung on my hand through the glove, I've taken the glove off, I can't see a stinger."

"Well done!" Vera had a quick look at the hand, it was red and swollen and there was no sign of the stinger.

"I'll call for help, stay very quietly where you are."

She ran into the kitchen found the phone and dialled 999,

"Emergency, which service?" said a calm man's voice.

"I don't really know! I am calling from the island of Strathsay, from the lighthouse. A man has been stung by a bee and is having trouble breathing. I'm not sure what to do! We need some help!"

"Help is on its way!" said the calm reassuring voice. "I have alerted the nurse, she is on her way to you as we speak. Leave him where he is, but most importantly keep him quiet. If you can see the sting try to remove it by scraping it off. Do not under any circumstance pinch it to pull it out, as that will squeeze the poison sack. Tell me is he breathing? What is his pulse? Is he conscious? Is he bleeding?"

"I don't know, I had to leave him to call for help, if the nurse is on her way I will go back to him. Thank you so much for your help."

Then she ran back out to him. He was still conscious when she got back to him, and he had not deteriorated any further. She was able to reassure him that the nurse was on her way and that everything would be ok as long as he just stayed quiet until she got there.

She looked at his glove. She could see the little poison sack, at the end of the stinger, which was embedded in the leather of the glove and also a long bit of bee intestine, which had been pulled out when the bee had stung him. It was a small consolation that it wouldn't be doing it again, as having used it's sting it would die. She took her hive tool and scraped the stinger off the glove.

"Hello'oh where are you?" Nurse Beth called down the garden,

"Over here by the shed" Vera stood up and waved. Beth was carrying a large red rucksack on her back,

"Hello Jimmy." Beth knelt down beside him, sliding the backpack off, and at the same time taking his wrist and automatically taking his pulse. Whilst she was quickly assessing the situation. "How are you?"

Jimmy nodded quietly from side to side and pouted his lips,

"Not so good?" Beth enquired,

He shook his head.

"He got stung through the glove, his eyes are ever so swollen."

"They sure are. Are you allergic to bees Jimmy?" Beth asked. He shook his head.

"I'll just give you a little injection of some antihistamine, ok?"

He nodded. She got the syringe ready, and gave him the injection. The swelling on the arm went all the way up to the elbow now, and the hand and forearm was red and very warm to the touch.

A few minutes after the injection Jimmy started to recover and pushed himself a bit up to a better position. And after a little while the two women helped him back up to the cottage, and settled him on the sofa. He continued to recover, and Beth asked if it was possible for Vera to stay with him overnight. Vera reassured her that that was absolutely no problem at all.

Beth gave Vera her telephone number, and said she would require Vera to count Jimmy's breathing and pulse every hour the next 6 hours, if he remained stable, nothing needed to happen, if he deteriorated he would have to be airlifted to the mainland to the hospital over there.

"Are you happy to stay? "

Beth double-checked, being well aware how scary it can be for someone who is not used to caring for others medically to be handed such a big responsibility. Yes, Vera felt she could manage, but it was reassuring that she could ring Beth if she was in doubt, Beth said she could be back very quickly if Vera needed her.

"I used to be a nurse, so I think I'll be alright. It's good to know that I can call on you though, and thank you so much for coming so quickly earlier."

"Aha!" Beth smiled. "That explains how you could be so calm, now I understand. It's a great help that I can leave you to look after him. How wonderful to have another nurse on the island. You just call if in doubt about anything, ok?"

Jimmy rested on the sofa, and Vera made a cold drink for him, and sat down. After a little while Jimmy fell asleep, Vera sat so she could see his breathing, it was nice and regular. As his colour was good too, she began to relax and wondered if it would be ok for her to disappear into the kitchen to make some food for dinner. Sirius being his good old self, was asleep right next to Jimmy, surely if he was happy and relaxed then Jimmy was ok?

But she couldn't convince herself that it was ok to leave the room, so she sat and counted his breathing for a few minutes. As it was completely steady, she went out in the kitchen, and had a look in the fridge. The bachelor's fridge was not equipped for many meals, so what could she make? It would have to be cheese on toast and then Battenberg cake for dessert, as she managed to find one in the larder.

She went back to check on her patient, he was still asleep, and looked fine. She prepared the evening meal for them, put it all on a tray, and brought it into the sitting room. The clinking of the teacups, woke him up and he lifted his head and smiled weakly,

"Phew! That was a bit of an ordeal"

"That was a good long sleep! How are you feeling Jimmy?"

"I've been better. My hand and arm is really itchy, but apart from that I think I'm ok."
He pushed himself up.

"Well you just take it easy now, I have prepared some tea, it is only cheese on toast, and Battenberg for dessert, I hope that's alright?"

"Oh, that is wonderful Vera and just what I fancied actually," he sent her a grateful smile.

"Where do I find food for Sirius?"

"It is in the cupboard next to the sink"

"How much shall I give him? And where is his bowl?

"One mug, and the bowl is in the food bag"

"OK. Is it ok to leave you for a little while whilst I feed the dog and let him out? Are you feeling alright now?"

"Yes thank you for all your concern, I am weak but feel fine now."

The phone rang, just as she went out into the kitchen with the tray with the empty plates. It was Beth checking up on the situation, she was pleased everything was fine, and pleased Vera had fed him and kept him quiet.

"Well done Vera, you really are a kind and good neighbour, and I can't thank you enough for looking after Jimmy."

"It's a pleasure." Vera felt good that Beth was happy with her nursing. She would need to speak to Beth about what they needed to do about the future, because obviously Jimmy was allergic to bees, so where did they go from here with regard to beekeeping? But for now that could wait.

Jimmy was happy to go to bed after tea, and Vera made herself comfortable on the sofa. She would be checking on Jimmy once an hour for several hours still, and sat the timer for an hour and snuggled down on the already warm sofa.

All night she checked on him every hour, and he continued to recover and actually slept soundly all night.

In the morning Vera felt like death warmed up. She remembered night duties and disturbed nights like this when Martin was poorly. It brought back really sad feelings that were difficult to shake off. She tried to keep busy and made some breakfast for them and fed Sirius and let him out. Beth rang at about eight o'clock and asked to the patient. She was very pleased that he had slept all night,

"And what about you Vera? I bet you feel rough this morning?" Well she didn't deny it, but reassured Beth that it was more important that Jimmy got better, she didn't have anything outstanding to see to, so she would just stay with Jimmy.

"I am going to pop by after surgery to check Jimmy's blood-pressure and his peak flow, is there anything that you are short of or need?"

Vera reassured Beth that all was under control and they were absolutely fine.

"Great! I shall see you later this morning then, and please remember, any changes, call me straight away. And before I go, thanks ever so much again for your amazing help."

"You're welcome, I am always happy to help!"
By the time Beth arrived, Jimmy was up, washed and dressed. The swelling of the eyes had gone down and

the redness of the arm was also nearly gone, but it was still a bit swollen and very itchy.

"You have made a good recovery Jimmy, I think we can let Nurse Vera go off duty now, don't you think?" She smiled at Vera.

"Well I have to admit I have rather enjoyed having her here, and it seems a shame if she has to go already…she ehh… is welcome to stay a bit longer."

"And I am very happy to stay a bit longer, Jimmy. But at some point it will be nice to brush my teeth and get into some clean clothes."

"Well then, how about if I call in late afternoon and do your checks again, then I can bring you back home Vera. How does that suit both of you?"

Jimmy and Vera exchanged glances and nodded, that was the perfect solution. And that was the reason that Vera came home to a cold house as the stoves had gone out. It was really miserable after so many hours of having company and even someone to care for too. And the sad memories of losing dear Martin lingered.

She got the stoves lit and made herself a sandwich and a bowl of soup. Then she ran a warm bath, and turned in, as it was a very long time since she had been this tired.

As she prepared for bed she thought how much she had enjoyed being a nurse again. She plugged in the mobile phone to charge it up, and much to her surprise she found a message from Lisa saying that she would love to come after Easter. What a lovely surprise! All tiredness disappeared immediately and she called her straight away. They were both so excited to be seeing each other again. It would only be for a few days, but a few days was better than not at all. So with great excitement she fell asleep whilst planning Lisa's visit and making mental lists.

Lisa arrived on the ferry on Good Friday morning and would sail back again on Monday. It was only a few days but they packed the days full of experiences and had such a great time together. They walked out to the lighthouse, where Jimmy was more than delighted to meet Lisa and show her around. Lisa had never been to a lighthouse and found it all absolutely fascinating. Lisa was full of praise for the island and Harbour View, and could really appreciate why Vera had been so drawn to the island.

This was the longest they had ever been apart since they shared a room in the nurses home all those years ago. My word! What they hadn't got up to in those days. They recalled the days and laughed at their antics.

They also shared some good food and a glass of wine, and talked until late. It had never been difficult for them to talk. Vera showed Lisa the plan for the vegetable garden, and Lisa was so impressed to see the potatoes already sprouting on the window sills. She fully understood why Vera loved it up here, and she reassured her that she would come often for sure!

# 31

It was the end of April, and the sun was getting stronger everyday and the days were lengthening noticeably. The summer birds were beginning to return to the island and there were frequent visitors at the bird table, which she had placed so she could see it from the kitchen window.

The vegetable garden and fruit bushes were all doing really well. And as soon as there were no more dangers of frost she had put the potatoes in the ground. She went to see to the chickens in the coop. She had got Henny and Hetty from her little friend Simon's chicken coop and they had become great pets. They were very tame and came when she called and they were excellent layers and had given her an egg each almost every day.

Sometimes there was one, sometimes two and other days none, it was a bit unreliable.

She had made the coop herself and painted it, duck-egg blue, it was rather gorgeous she thought. She had laughed at that name when she chose the colour. She had bought it flat-packed, but even so she was proud of her achievement. The nesting box at the back had a lid that she could open from the outside. She could reach straight down and collect her daily eggs. She had given the chucks an old broom handle to perch on inside the coop.

The front opened completely so it was easy to clean the coop out. She scattered sawdust on the floor, and put clean straw in the nesting boxes once a week. All the sweepings went on the compost.

She filled the water container and poured corn in the feeder, after scattering a bit on the ground for the ladies to pick at. She had been in the garden most of the afternoon and she was quite tired after the evening meal and decided to retire to bed early with her tea and a good book.

She was fast asleep when the telephone woke her. Startled, she looked at the alarm clock which said it was only 3.13 am, '*who on earth would be ringing me at this ungodly hour',* she thought as she stumbled out of bed, grabbing her dressing gown as she went into the sitting room, finding the phone. *'This will either be bad news or a wrong number'*, she picked up the receiver and answered hesitatingly.

It was Nurse Beth, she had been called to the neighbours house, unfortunately Simon's mum Emma had gone into labour much too early. Beth was going to be driving past Vera's house on her way to them, could she possibly pick her up and bring her to the neighbours house? Karl and Emma were wondering whether Vera would look after little Simon whilst the three of them flew to the hospital on the mainland in the emergency helicopter, which had already been scrambled and was on its way. Of course she would only be too pleased to help, and quickly got dressed. She was standing by the gate when the nurse arrived in her Land-Rover, and together they drove round the headland to Karl and Emma's house.

The lights were on in the whole house. Emma was in bed, her waters had broken, and contractions had started soon afterwards. She was only 32 weeks pregnant, which was much too early for a little baby to be born, especially at home. The danger was that it might have breathing problems, because of the immature lungs. So the decision was easily made that they had to go to hospital. Simon was awake sitting in the bed snuggled up with his mum, he fully understood that mum and dad had to go. He was of course upset at the prospect of being left, but he appeared to be very reassured that Vera would look after him. Mum was giving directions where to find this and that. Vera made a list of all the things she needed to know, school times, school uniform, sports bag, music bag, and lunch box. She made notes of Simon's favourites for breakfast, lunch and dinner. What was allowed and not allowed. Children's television programs were out of bounds, *thank goodness I don't have a TV* she thought. She was really looking forward to looking after Simon, and so pleased that the little family had incorporated her into their midst so early on that Simon now was comfortable with her.

Fortunately Emma had already got baby clothes, nappies and toiletries ready, but the clothes were for a new-born baby, not a tiny little premature one, so they would all be much too big. The helicopter arrived. It was incredibly noisy, and then it flew hastily away with its precious cargo. Vera and Simon stood on the doorstep and waved goodbye, and once the flashing light had disappeared, they went inside. Vera put a bit of wood on the fire, and turned the kettle on again. It didn't take long to boil, it was still warm from the many cups that had been made in the night, and made them both a hot drink.

"I think we better have hot chocolate, on an exciting night like this we need something warm and sweet, don't you think Simon?" He nodded energetically. Hot chocolate in the middle of the night! Maybe this was not too bad after all.

Thoughts of her beloved Grandma flooded in again, as she and Simon snuggled up on the sofa. They sat together under a lovely colourful patchwork blanket, which Emma had made, talking about the happenings of the night. Simon was reassured and wanted to have a look at his favourite storybook, the one about Alfie and Annie-Rose. Simon had heard the story hundreds of times before and knew it off by heart, but still he loved hearing it again and again. He felt safe and warm with Vera and very soon he dozed off again, and so did Vera.

Later she felt little movements next to her. She was a bit disorientated at first, but soon remembered where she was and what had happened. Keeping as quiet as a mouse, she hardly dared to breathe, not to wake Simon. She thought that she would just let him come to gently and slowly. *'I'll just let him realise he is waking up on the sofa and not in his own bed and let him wonder a bit about how that can be, and then let the memories of last night slowly come back. I will make some little reassuring noises, and hopefully he will snuggle up and we can talk about last night again.'*

She had judged him exactly right, so as they sat together, he in his pj's and she fully clothed from last night, the sky was pink and the sun was up. Simon wanted to know when mum and dad would come home, and Vera reassured him that they would definitely be returning, but that it was very difficult to give a precise day or even time, they would just have to be very patient and said,

"Let's thank God for this brand new day, and ask him to keep mum, dad and baby safe."

Then they chatted about the baby, would it be a boy or a girl? Simon thought it would be great to have a little sister, some of his friends at school had sisters and they were such fun. They had different toys, dolls and prams, which Simon had enjoyed playing with when visiting friends. Vera got an idea, how about if we ask to borrow a doll and a pram and a few baby things, then we can practise for when mummy brings the new baby home. Simon thought that would be a great idea. Alfie had a little sister in the book too, so they chatted a bit more about what it would be like becoming a big brother.

Vera explained that not a lot would change really, mum and dad and Simon would still be as they had always been, but mum would be more tired, as she would be feeding the baby, and she would wake up several times a night to do so.

"So it is important to be helpful and understanding, and I will also try to help you and mum as much as I can, and if you want to come to my house to play a bit more often, then I could maybe fetch you from school…School!" Vera suddenly remembered and looked at the time.

"Well I suppose we better get a move on, let's get going Simon, and find your uniform and have some breakfast. Simon said that they also had to remember to let the chickens out and collect the eggs. Vera filled the kettle and put it on the AGA, Simon went to get dressed and put his wellington boots on. They were funny green ones that looked like a frog with great big yellow bulging eyes and big red smiling lips on the noses of the boots.'*What fun!* 'Vera thought to herself, why not make some fun out of otherwise boring wellies. Then he picked up the tin of chicken food and the basket for the eggs, Vera put on her coat, and off they went. It was a bright but chilly morning. The chickens were all inside the coop, the enclosure where they could roam was huge, there was a grassy area and also a patch of bare ground, Vera asked how come, and Simon answered all Vera's questions very knowledgeably.

"Dad keeps moving the fence so there is always a fresh piece of grass for them, if you look over there you can see that is the old patch from last week." Vera admitted that she didn't know an awful lot about chickens and was still learning, and was very impressed by the little boy's knowledge. They opened the door and let the chucks out. They were pleased and were shaking their wings and plumage and the cockerel immediately flew up on the top of the coop and announced that he and his chicks were now out and about. He strutted about, looking so proud and his long tail feathers were gleaming and shimmering in the sun and the comb on top of his head was bright red.

Simon opened the lid to the nesting area, and found 5 newly laid eggs, which were still warm. Memories of her times with Grannie again came back. How amazing! Fancy a little child being brought up like this in this day and age. Her own children had never even seen a chicken coop, she didn't think, trying to think back.

Simon gathered the eggs carefully in the basket so as not to crack the shells. He then threw food on the ground for the chickens to peck and filled the feeder and the water bowl. They went inside again, this whole thing had taken less than five minutes. He didn't need help getting dressed, he could even do up shoelaces he proudly announced, and showed her how he did it. They always wore felt slippers in the house and boots outside. Vera made toast and a poached egg for them, and after breakfast they picked up the satchel, and the packed lunch that mum had been so organised and made the night before and put in the fridge. Vera looked in it, there was a sandwich, and some chopped carrots and cucumber, and an apple.

## 32

Then they set off to school, Simon was happy, he hopped skipped and jumped along. They walked past Harbour View and Vera changed her shoes to boots. They got to the little bridge and Vera asked Simon if he had ever played Pooh-sticks, which he never had, so Vera promised she would show him on the way home when she fetched him from school later on.

There was great excitement in the playground, several children were playing around kicking a ball, two girls were standing at the tree playing a clapping game, and they were giggling like only girls can do, whilst reciting a rhyme. Some of the children had heard the helicopter in the night, and they were talking about what could have happened. They all gathered round Simon when he entered the playground, to hear his news.

Vera went across the playground and knocked on the door to the classroom and entered the large airy and bright room, leaving Simon in the playground. The teacher had filled the wood-burning stove and the room was lovely and warm. She was busy making preparations for today's lessons, she turned towards Vera, smiled and came towards her. Vera introduced herself again even though they had met at the beekeeping afternoon, and explained the circumstances at Simon's house, and that she would be fetching and bringing Simon to school for a few days, at least until the little family was reunited again.

The teacher was a delightful middle-aged lady, with the nicest personality. Vera had liked her immediately when they met the first time. She had no doubt that this school was absolutely fantastic with a lady like Mrs Mac Donald in charge. She commanded respect in the nicest possible way. She said she would let Vera know if there was anything she needed to know, and help her with advice if she needed it. She told Vera that every child would bring homework every day, and reminded her of the importance of it.

Mrs Mac Donald would leave information for Vera in the notebook that was kept in the satchel, and asked if she would kindly put any information in there that she thought would be helpful for school to know about. As she said, maybe Simon wouldn't sleep so well if he was worried about his parents, and it would be important for her to know of all circumstances that would or could be affecting him. So they agreed to let each other know of any changes. Vera thanked her for her help and pointed out that it was after all a few days since she had been bringing children to school and surely things would have changed over the years.

She went back out to Simon, who was already involved in a game with some boys. When he saw Vera, he ran over to her and said,

"This is my best friend Neil, he also has chickens, but he only got 4 eggs this morning" Vera laughed and said,

"Hello Neil, I'm sure we'll be seeing more of you soon, does your mum come to fetch you?" Neil answered that she always did, so Vera said she would look forward to meeting her this afternoon at the gate and with that she bid them goodbye just as Mrs Mac Donald came out and rang the big hand-bell,

"Time to come inside, line up. Please."

Vera noticed with delight how she then proceeded to greet each child: "Good-morning Johnny, nice haircut! Good-morning Susie, lovely ribbons!" and so on, and to Simon she said "I can't wait to hear *your* news! Simon"

Vera walked by the post office on her way home and called in to let them know that Karl and Emma had gone to the hospital, so to keep any post waiting for them. Mrs M was ever so concerned, and told Vera to pass on their very best regards.

Getting back home Vera realised how tired she was. She took off her clothes and jumped into bed after lighting the wood burners.

*'I shall have to keep my strength up to cope with this, so better be ahead and sleep before I get too tired.'*

And with that she snuggled into bed, but found it hard to sleep when it was so light outside. So she snoozed thinking about Karl and Emma, hoping to get some news soon.

She also worried about Nurse Beth, how was she going to get back to the island. Eventually she managed to drop off to sleep only to be woken by a knock on the door. It was Brendan, Beth's husband; he had walked over to fetch the land-rover, and called in on the way back to say that they had arrived safely at the hospital, and so far so good. Vera inquired to Beth, how was she going to get back?

"She will arrive back on the ferry this lunch time. I'll fetch her, hence I need the car." Vera apologised for being in her dressing gown at eleven in the morning,

"Well you've had a bit of a night I understand, so no worries" he smiled warmly, said goodbye and went off again.

Vera decided to get up. She was going to get a meal on the way for Simon. She would make spaghetti bolognese, which always was a winner with him.

The phone went as she was just frying the onions. She took the pan off the hot plate and closed the lid, wiped her hands and answered the phone. It was Karl,

"Hello Vera, how are you getting on? Did you get Simon off to school all right, were there any problems?

"None whatsoever" Vera reassured him. "But Karl, how are things with you and Emma? I heard from Beth's husband that you got to the hospital ok, how are things now?"

"Well, we're delighted to tell you that we've had a beautiful little baby girl, (Vera could hear that he was smiling) we have called her Rosie, she only weighed 3lb3oz, so she is very tiny. She has been to the breast and sucked really well for such a tiny little mite. But she must not get too exhausted sucking so Emma will have to express milk too and give her that as well. Oh Vera, we are so relieved! And thank you so much for looking after Simon, it is an enormous help."

"Oh congratulations Karl," Vera felt tears on her cheeks, and wiped them off with the back of her hand. "Is Emma all right? Was the birth fairly easy? What time was she born? How long is she?" All the questions came tumbling out; she had been so worried for the little family.

Karl calmly reassured her that all was well, and that Emma was fine, the birth had been straight forward, and Rosie was born at twenty past eight, he couldn't remember how long she was, but she was *adorable*, his proud father-heart was full to burst. They would have to stay in the hospital until they were sure the tiny mite was thriving, they had been told that she would most likely get jaundiced as most premature babies did. Being jaundiced could make the baby drowsy and therefore not so interested in feeding, but once over that hurdle, the doctor had said they could most likely go home.

Vera wished them all well, and asked if Karl would contact people on the island himself. He said he would really appreciate it if Vera would let everyone know.

"Perhaps you could help Simon make a birth announcement for the notice board?" Karl suggested and Vera thought that it was a great idea, and promised to see to it.

They rang off, and Vera went back to the dinner preparations, once she had browned the onions and the meat, she added the tinned tomatoes, the chopped celery and spices, placed the lid on the top of the casserole dish and put it in the simmering oven.

'*Well this calls for a celebration*' she thought, and made a lovely little dessert in a ramekin, which she decorated with a pink ribbon. She went outside and found some little spring flowers and placed them on the table. *'Rosie'*, she thought, *'what a beautiful name for a little baby girl.'*

She was so excited when she walked down to the school to fetch Simon. Going past the post office she popped in to Mrs M and told her the news and that she was going to make a birth announcement with Simon to put on the notice board.

There were a few mums at the gate, Vera asked who was Neil's mum, the mums smiled and pointed to a lady who came driving a quad bike along the track. She has a sheep dog in the back wearing a bandana smartly round its neck. She pulled up towards the gate, turned off the engine, hopped off the vehicle, telling the dog to stay, and came over and joined the other women. Ella, Susie's mum who Vera had met this morning said,

"Hi Caroline, I don't think you have met Vera, have you? Vera lives at Harbour View she only moved in in March, she's the one with the bees, ye nooh'. Vera, this is Caroline."

They shook hands, Caroline said that she usually came to the school a different way, but today she had an errand and therefore came past Vera's house.

She had the most amazing red curly hair that blew wildly around her head, as she zoomed along. She had red cheeks and a smattering of freckles over her nose and she wore old-fashioned little round 'gold rimmed' glasses and a very colourful knitted pullover. Vera liked Caroline straight away. She lived on the other side of the second headland, past Karl and Emma's, she was a sheep farmer. She had been born and bred on the island, and had taken over the running of the farm, when her dad fell and broke his hip whilst out herding sheep on the moor several years ago. He was still alive but didn't do much on the farm any more.

"I am going past yours on the way home, so maybe I can give you a lift?" Vera explained that she was here to fetch Simon, and that Simon had told her that Neil was his best friend,

"I was actually going to ask if Neil would be able to come home with Simon to play one day.

Caroline thought that was a great idea, "Would tomorrow be a good day? I'll tell you why, she said,

"I have to take dad for a check up at the doctors, she is coming tomorrow, and the appointment is at 2.30pm, so if you could possibly fetch the boys and bring them to Harbour View that would be a great help. Then I can bring dad back home and fetch Neil afterwards."

So that was agreed, no problem at all.

## 33

When the children came out Vera smiled and nodded at the head mistress and gave a wink and a thumbs up, Mrs Mac Donald smiled back and nodded, *'I think she understood that message at least I hope so'.*

Vera did not say anything to the mothers about why she was fetching Simon, she thought she would let Simon be the bearer of the great news from his family.

They all hopped on to the back of the quad bike, Jess, the dog, made room for them. It was a rather bumpy and uncomfortable ride, but the boys loved it. They squealed and laughed, all the way back to Harbour View, where Vera and Simon jumped out.

"Thank you ever so much for the lift! Please let the school know I am fetching Neil tomorrow Caroline, and I look forward to seeing you later then, and good luck with your dad's appointment. Bye-bye."

Simon was tired, it had been an exciting day. He'd had to tell them all about his mum, and the helicopter, and the new baby that had decided to come much too early. Vera made them a cup of tea and a sandwich, and they sat down at the table, and Vera listened to all his news.

"I have made spaghetti bolognaise for dinner," Simon looked up at her with big eyes. He wanted to laugh but had just bitten off a big mouthful of sandwich. He chewed and swallowed it quickly,

"You've made spaghetti for me? Yeayhhhh it *IS* my lucky day!" he exclaimed.

"It is indeed your lucky day today Simon. I have some very special news for you. Daddy rang just before I went to the school to fetch you"

"Yeees" said Simon with an inquisitive expression,

"What did he say, are they coming home?"

"He said that you have got a tiny little baby sister called Rosie,"

Vera smiled, her eyes welling up with happy tears. Well! This was just too much for a little five year old, on top of such an exciting night and special day. Simon could not contain himself, he jumped down from the table and danced around in small circles, shouting hurrah, and threw himself round Vera's neck and hugged her,

"A baby sister! My very own baby sister! Rosie! What a great name! When are they coming home?" Vera sat him on her lap and explained how they would both have to be very patient as Rosie was so small, and that it would be a little while before mum and dad would bring Rosie back to the island. Simon understood perfectly. He had seen the tiny chickens in the coop, seen how the mother kept them under the wings to protect them until they were big enough to venture out.

He thought it was a great idea to make the poster and wanted to set to work straight away. Vera cleared the tea away so he had the use of the table, and found paper and crayons. And together they made a brilliant colourful poster announcing Rosie's arrival. They would put it on the notice board on the way to school tomorrow.

"We must not forget to close up the chickens." Simon looked out of the window, the sun was setting, Vera had forgotten all about them and quickly went out to shut up her own two.

"Well done Simon, we better get going straight away then, actually now you have made the poster we can go back to your house and stay the night there. She took the bolognaise out of the oven, and put some in a container, which she wrapped in a big towel and put it all in a big shopping bag. She packed an overnight bag and then they put on their clothes and walked over to Simon's house.

It was still light enough to see when they got there but the chickens had already retired for the night, so it was just a question of closing the door to the coop. They went into the dark house, took off their boots and coats, and went into the living room. The wood burners had gone out, but Simon knew all about how to lay the fire and soon the flames danced happily behind the glass doors, and the AGA had kept the house fairly warm too. Vera cooked the spaghetti and with-in half an hour they could sit down to a nourishing meal. Simon tucked in as if he hadn't seen food for a week; Vera was pleased she had given him the sandwich in the afternoon. She had forgotten all about the celebration desserts, which now sat waiting happily in the fridge…*'well there is also tomorrow '* she thought.

Simon was so tired that he asked to go to bed straight after dinner. '*There will be no homework tonight'* Vera thought to herself as she tucked the sleepy little boy in, but I am sure that is all right; it is after all not every day one becomes a big brother. *'And notice to self: I better be a lot more organised, if this is going to last a few weeks.'* She thought that tomorrow she would ask if Caroline would mind to close Simon's chickens up, on her way past when she fetched Neil. She made a bed for herself on the sofa, kept the doors open so she could hear Simon. She cleared up in the kitchen, and went to bed, she was not far from being as exhausted as little Simon.

## 34

The next morning it rained. It was one of these dark and dank drizzly days that she disliked so much as it never seemed to get light. The raindrops gathered and made rivulets on the window pane. Simon made a competition game with them whilst having breakfast.

They had been out to the chickens, who had not been too keen to get out, but at least the door was open and they could get out if they wanted to. This morning there were six eggs.

"What are we going to do with all these eggs Simon? We can't possibly eat so many." Simon suggested they brought them to school.

"Sometimes the cook will bake us a cake if we bring eggs in". Vera asked what he would like for breakfast and in his packed lunch today, they had a look in the fridge together and he decided he would like a cheese sandwich, a yoghurt and an orange for lunch and a boiled egg for breakfast.

Simon's wellies were completely muddy and they'd had to be left outside the back door, until it was time to go to school. They put his slippers in the satchel as Simon informed Vera that wellies had to be left in the cloakroom at school. When they got to the little brook, they washed them easily by just standing in the water.

"We never got to play pooh sticks did we, if it isn't raining when we walk home with Neil this afternoon, we can do it then. Hey, what do you think Neil would like as a snack when we get home from school? Do you think a homemade roll and hot chocolate would be a good idea?"

Simon definitely thought that would be a brilliant idea. So off to school they trotted, they brought the new baby poster to the post office on the way. Mrs M was so excited that she came round the counter and hugged Simon and congratulated him on becoming a big brother and promised to put it on the notice board straight away, and gave him some little packs of raisins to give to his classmates to celebrate the good news. Vera said they were bringing in the eggs too and maybe the cook would bake a cake!

"Noooh-doubt-about-it!" exclaimed Mrs M smiling broadly "and if you have more eggs than you can manage, I will sell them for you. Just write the date they were laid on the shell with a pencil. No problem, they are always sought after, not everybody has chickens."

They watched as Mrs M put the poster up, it took pride of place on the notice board. Several people had seen it and on the way back from school, everyone they met congratulated Simon. He was as proud as punch and somehow seemed to have grown a bit taller!

Cook had indeed baked a cake, and because there had been too many raisin packets, she had been able to put raisins in the cake too and it had been extremely yummy. They had it for dessert with custard. What a treat it had been. They had talked about children and babies most of the day, they had learnt about where babies came from, how they grew in the womb inside the mummy's tummy,

"For NINE months!! That is a looooong time," said Simon" just think how long the summer holiday is and it is longer than that!" Simon was chatting as they ambled home after school with Neil. They played pooh sticks at the brook and they had great fun, throwing them in and racing over to the other side of the bridge to see whose stick came out first. From this they soon learnt that the water moves fastest in the middle of the stream.

The hot chocolate and the freshly baked rolls were a great success, and Vera showed them how to dunk! But Vera said,

"This is only allowed here at Harbour View, as it is not really good manners,"

And she certainly didn't want them to go to school and start dunking there, saying that she had taught them to do it. What would Mrs Mac Donald not think?

The boys laughed as the little yellow fat pearls from the melted butter scuttled around on the top of the chocolate, they loved the rolls, and ate two each.

"I hope this won't spoil your appetite for dinner, I have a little celebration dessert from yesterday which we forgot to eat, I hope you'll like it" They munched them too with great gusto. Afterwards they played, 'hide the thimble', they had to direct each other to the hiding place. They were very inventive in their hiding places, and the three of them had great fun. When Caroline came to fetch Neil, Vera invited her for a cup of tea, she too was delighted with the home made roll. She said it was the tastiest roll she had had in a very long time.

"It is my fathers recipe, he used to bake them and so did my Grannie." She told Caroline that she had showed the boys how to dunk! Caroline was laughing!

"Hweeel ne-uh aiii neverrrrr" Wot arrr yee teachin' tham?"

"Well, it won't do them any harm and they know it is only to be done here at my house and nowhere else, isn't that right boys?" The boys nodded energetically totally agreeing with Vera. It was nice to be allowed to be naughty!

Caroline would drive past Simon's house on the way back and shut up the chickens. Neil thanked Vera for a nice afternoon and she replied that she hoped he would like to come again another time.

# 35

The next day Vera decided that although it was farther to walk everyday it would be easier for everyone if they stayed at Simon's house. She could see to her own chickens on the way home from school. So she packed a rucksack with things she would need, she could always come back for more once she had brought Simon to school. When Karl rang she told him of the plan which he was in total agreement with. They decided Karl should ring to Simon in the afternoon at their house, she told him they were usually there about four o'clock and,

"He will be very pleased to hear your voice," she said.

"But please don't be upset if he starts crying when he hears your voice." Vera explained why she was so sure that would happen.

When she fetched Simon she asked him how he would feel if they stayed at his house instead of at Harbour View, she explained how she felt it was easier because of the chickens and they could shut up Vera's on the way home and also then Simon would have his toys around him. Simon didn't mind at all, he was happy at both places. He was very excited to hear that dad would be calling him in the afternoon.

On the way home they talked about how mum and Rosie were doing. Simon was missing his parents, Vera could tell, as he had become rather quiet. She had prepared herself that there might be tears when Simon spoke to his dad. So she took the opportunity to talk a bit about missing people, and how when we hear the voice of someone we miss, we can sometimes get a bit upset, as it reminds us how much we miss them, but that it feels good to speak and be reassured that all is well at the other end. She explained it well and in a reassuring way, and he understood. It was very obvious to Vera that Simon's parents spoke to him in a very grown up way.

"So what are you going to tell dad about when he rings? Have you got anything exciting to tell him?" She looked down at him as they walked side by side. He looked up at her and smiled, and his little hand sneaked into hers. That moved Vera close to tears.

"I am going to tell him about the poster, and the pooh-sticks and the trip in the quad-bike." Then he thought for a moment," Do you think I should tell him about 'dunking'?"

She smiled to herself and said that as it was something only to be done at Harbour View, they could easily wait to tell that bit!

As predicted, as soon as Simon heard his Dad's voice tears welled up in his eyes. She sat next to him at the table and gently levered him over onto her lap and put her arms reassuringly around his little body. Karl kept talking, he was telling Simon about Rosie and mum, telling him about nappies and feeding, what Rosie looked like and the noises she made.

"Does she cry a lot?" Simon asked, as one of the boys at school had told how his baby sister had been crying and how the family had found it very upsetting, as they didn't seem to be able to comfort the baby except when she was breastfeeding. The boy had said he was annoyed as that meant that mum couldn't play with him so much.

"No darling she doesn't cry, she is with mum all the time, and as soon as she wakes mum feeds her. She has many little feeds. If Mum is sleeping I sit with her on my tummy, it is very important that she feels our skin and is kept warm all the time, so no Simon we don't let her cry at all." Karl was very reassuring.

"When are you coming home Daddy?"

"We are coming home as soon as we can Simon, I promise, but Rosie has to get over these first few days and then we will see, ok? But I promise that as soon as we possibly can we will come back. Are you ok little man?"

"Yes, we are fine," he looked up at Vera with his eyes questioning,

"Shall I tell him?" and she nodded, go ahead. He wiped his tears with the back of his hand and off he went telling of all the adventures, Karl laughed and Vera could hear that he was reassured that his little boy was doing fine in Vera's capable care.

They rang off and Vera noticed that the long phone call had made a difference. He seemed calmer and more settled. He did his homework with a smile. She found the little notice book in the satchel, yes there was a bit of reading and also a few sums. The children were learning a song for the end of term, and Mrs Mac Donald wanted all parents to practise it with the children.

When Simon was settled with his work at the dining table, Vera got on with the evening meal preparation, and once that was finished she sat down to hear him read. He did very well for his age. Once finished they went out to shut the chickens up for the night. Simon had a great appetite for dinner, he then had his bath and good night story and off he went to bed, after yet another exciting day.

And so the days went on until one day about 5 weeks later when Karl rang to announce that the little family would be arriving home on the ferry on the coming Friday. Would Vera be so kind as to put another poster on the notice board to say that they were coming home, and that everyone was welcome to pop in to welcome Rosie home but not between 12-15 when mother and baby would be resting. So Simon was given the task of using his creative skills once more, and made yet another colourful poster.

"Would you like to make a welcome home card to mum and Rosie?" Vera asked. Simon thought that would be a great idea and went to work at it straight away.

The day the family arrived home on the ferry, lots of islanders and all the children from the school went to meet the ferry with flags, and they all shouted "hurrah!!" when the little baby was carried ashore, and the family was showered with home made gifts and cards to welcome them home. Nurse Beth was there at the ready with the land-rover, which had been decorated with flowers, and Vera and Simon had made bunting to make the house pretty too. Simon was given the afternoon off school, this occasion was just so amazing and every one was so happy for the little family. Vera had made a lovely quiche and salad for the family, and hitched a lift back to Harbour View in the land-rover, where she hopped out and left the little family now reunited again to get home together. She reassured them that she was only a phone call away and that she would be happy to help with anything at all.

She waved happily good-bye as the land-rover pulled away, and went back inside...it *did* seem empty now without Simon. She had been home in the morning and lit the wood burners, so the house was lovely and warm now, which made it a bit easier. Being May the temperature outside was warmer as it took some time for the house to warm up. The thick walls not only protected from the cold. She had just put the kettle on when there was a knock on the door, and to her surprise she found Nurse Beth outside.

"May I come in for a moment?"

"Of course you can," Vera opened the door fully, "I have just put the kettle on, do you have time for a cuppa?"

So the two women sat and chatted for a little while, Beth would have to get back to 'the doctors house' in case anyone needed her, but she really came to thank Vera for stepping in and helping when it was most needed.

"You have been a tremendous help to the little family, and it has been more important than you will ever know. Because if Emma and Karl had been worrying and anxious about anything at home, it could easily have had an adverse effect on the breast feeding and Emma's well being and recovery." She took a sip and carried on, "and because you have helped the breastfeeding was quickly well established and they have been able to leave hospital much earlier than expected as the little mite is thriving beautifully. So do not belittle your efforts, this will have implications long into this little girl's life and for the family as a whole, so I really cannot thank you enough."

Vera blushed, she felt embarrassed to be praised so much. She had only done what she thought anyone would have done in the same situation, and she had been so pleased to be asked, and told Beth how she had come to love the little boy and what a delight he had been to look after.

"Thank you for asking me" she said smiling to Beth "if I can ever be of any help again don't hesitate to ask will you."

"I might very well have to call on you another time and it is very good to know that you are willing to help, so many thanks for the tea and the chat. They finished the tea talking about other things, and as Beth was a very busy lady, she was soon on her way again.

"Thanks again and see you soon!"
And with a wave she went off in the land-rover. The following day Beth rang Vera.

"I have had a think Vera. You said that you used to be a nurse. How would you consider coming to help me in the surgery? I could really do with a helper who knows what she is doing. You don't have to give me an answer straight away, but if you would please consider coming to give me a hand, I would really appreciate it."

"But I am not registered as a nurse anymore." Vera replied, but her brain raced - what an amazing opportunity it would be to get back into nursing.

"No, maybe not, but the knowledge is still there and you are extremely good at keeping calm and you have a lovely reassuring way about you. You won't have to do any nursing as such, but if you would be my extra hands, especially when I have sterile gloves on, answering the phone and things like that."

"Well I did think, when I met you the very first day that this must be the jewel in the crown of nursing like you do, cradle to grave. I think I can say yes now! I loved my nursing, but due to my slipped disc I had to give hospital nursing up. But working as your helper would be lovely, I would love to say yes please to the offer."

"The surgery is Tuesday and Thursday from 10-12, not set in stone and we can play it by ear. It will be great to have you on board. "

"When would you like me to start?" Vera asked.

"As soon as you can really." Beth replied

"Ok, well I shall see you on Tuesday then." Vera was thrilled.

And this is how Vera rekindled her love of nursing and she proved to be a fantastic helper for Beth. Soon other jobs were also delegated to Vera, but she particularly enjoyed being the one who could hold someone's hand if a dressing had to be changed, or stitches removed. Sometimes it was going on a home visit, maybe giving support to someone caring for an elderly relative or a sick child, or just delivering medicine. Or just holding the fort whilst Beth was phoning someone with some results or speaking to the doctor with a referral. The partnership between the two of them worked really well, and Beth was so pleased to have a competent helper that she could rely on.

# 36

She had retired early after a busy day of chopping and stacking wood and working in the garden and was fast asleep when something suddenly woke her. It felt like she was not alone in the room. She was lying very comfortably on her side with only her head above the soft duvet. She was scared! Her heart was hammering and she didn't dare to move. She opened her left eye, just a little tiny slit, just enough to see the friendly glow behind the glass of the wood stove.

*'Don't be silly now'*; she told herself. *'Who on earth would come in here in the middle of the night? You have probably just dreamt something.'* She was trying very hard to be sensible.

Even so she lay absolutely still for a little while, and listened intensely to the sounds in the house. The wind whistled and howled in the chimneys and the house was taking a real battering. Then a floorboard creaked, and that made her sit up with a jolt.

At the end of the bed stood a squat little old woman silhouetted against the dim light from the window. She was wrapped in a shawl, from her head, down over her shoulders and tucked in under her arms. It made her look almost cone shaped.

"Excuse me! Who are you?" Vera reached out and turned on the light, without taking her eyes off the woman. It seemed as if she was hugging herself tightly. Her back was bent; and she was leaning slightly forwards. She appeared almost see-through. Vera shook her head in disbelief.

Even though Vera was frightened at first, she quickly realised that the old woman was not a threat.

In a very strong Scottish accent the old woman said,

"I'm so sorry to wake ye Dear, but I do have something ye need to help me with."

The little woman's voice sounded gentle and friendly, even though Vera did not recognise her.

"What is the matter? What is it you need help with in the middle of the night?"

"No Dear, I am sorry but this is urgent. Ye see my time here is very short. I have been trying to get hold of you so often since you moved in, but this is the first time I have been lucky."

Vera tried to think back, she had absolutely no recollection of this woman trying to get in contact,

"I'm really sorry to hear that, how have you tried to contact me? I don't remember it."

"I have helped you find things. Do you remember when you found the little key in the woodshed and wondered where that would fit? I'd put it there for you to find."

"Oh yes I do remember! I've kept it. It is hanging on the wall in the kitchen; it is such a beautiful key. Have you come to get it back?" Vera lifted the corner of the duvet, to get out of bed, but the old lady lifted her hand in a gesture to stop her. She closed her eyes and shook her head sadly. Vera could see that she was getting upset as she hurriedly wiped a tear from her cheek.

"Right," Vera said assertively. "Let me go to make us a cup of tea, then you can tell me, what it is that needs to be done?"

"No thank ye Dear, ye are very kind. Listen!" She pointed upwards with a gnarled index finger, "in the cupboard under the eves, there is a loose floorboard, under it ye'll find a small wooden box. The key fits that lock." And with that she just seemed to evaporate! She was gone and the room was empty again.

Vera could not believe her eyes and sat astonished in the bed for a few minutes; she was actually rather shaken up by the whole unbelievable experience. She was not really quite sure if this really had happened or had she in fact dreamt it all.

The whole thing with the key that kept appearing all the time had made her doubt her sanity on several occasions, and now this was added to the strangeness of it all. She decided to get up. She put on her dressing gown and warm slippers and looked at the time. It was just the midnight hour and that spooked her more than anything.

She went out into the kitchen and put the kettle on. Not for a cup of tea this time, no this definitely called for hot chocolate.

Vera talked to herself, mostly to calm herself down; it had been a very strange experience indeed. Whilst waiting for the kettle to boil she put a couple of logs on the fire.

"I can't really believe this," she said out loud, rustling her hair with her hands, as if to get the thoughts out of her head. "It's so unreal, yet she was so convincing, such a dear little old lady. I should have asked her name, shouldn't I? She seemed *so* convincing and real! How could she suddenly disappear into thin air like that?" she poured the boiling water on the chocolate powder, "I'll go up and check that cupboard out. Then I'll know if it was just something I dreamt."

She went upstairs with a torch. She turned all the lights on too, and went to the cupboard the old woman had mentioned.

Yes! There certainly was a loose floorboard, but if no one had told her she would never have found it. She lifted it and there, tucked away was a beautiful wooden box. Vera lifted it out carefully. It was very dusty and had obviously been there a very long time. She replaced the floorboard carefully before closing the cupboard, and brought the box downstairs.

She sat down on the sofa with it. It was tied up with a platted woollen string the same as on the key. It was obviously a very old wooden box. It was about the same size as a modern cardboard shoebox, but beautifully made with dovetailed corners and inlaid wood in an intricate pattern. Somebody had taken very great care in making it. Vera was reluctant to open it, unsure of what she might find.

She sipped the hot chocolate, it wouldn't matter if she waited until the morning, would it?

The hot chocolate was soothing and warmed her; she turned off all the lights and went back into the bedroom leaving the box on the sofa. She would open it in the morning.

The bed was still warm and she snuggled down into its comforting safety. She would call Jimmy in the morning and ask him to pop in.

She tossed and turned the rest of the night and woke up feeling very uneasy. Just before she woke she had a very weird dream about her Dad. She could see his lips move, but could not hear what he was saying. She had not been able to make him understand that she wasn't able to hear him. It somehow felt urgent, as if he had something pressing to tell her.

At five o'clock she gave up and decided to get up. It felt as if she hadn't slept at all.

Her whole body ached but that was most probably more due to the wood chopping yesterday rather than the lack of sleep. She made some toast and a cup of tea.

The box was still sitting there on the sofa. Intriguingly. She was in no obvious hurry to open it. She would deal with it when Jimmy could be there.

The blustery wind from yesterday had eased, and although it was still dark outside, there was no howling in the chimneys and the fires were again burning steadily.

Sunrise was imminent and it felt a lot calmer everywhere. Hopefully it would be nice enough to be outside again today.

"Uhhh." She shuddered, it had been such a spooky night and she had goose pimples all over just thinking about it all.

She decided enough was enough and tried to put the experience behind her for the time being and ran the bath as usual. But the feeling of urgency from the dream wouldn't leave her, what could it be that her Dad had been trying to tell her?

It turned out to be a really dricht day. That's what they called a dark dank wet day up here, and not a day to be outside so why not see if she could calm this urgent feeling inside her, by trying to find some facts about her Dad. After breakfast she decided that she would do some research on the computer. She knew that her Dad had been adopted, but had never investigated anything about it.

She'd hardly got it turned on before there was a knock at the door.

It was Jimmy! That was lucky! She had forgotten that she wanted to ring to him. He said that he too had been up very early, and that he was on his way to the post office and did she need anything? She invited him in for a cup of tea, and they sat and chatted for a while. He noticed the beautiful box on the sofa. She told him of the night's visit and the uneasy feeling the dream had left her with.

"It sounds to me as if you could do with some fresh air to clear that old brain of yours! Why don't you put your boots on and walk with me?" He said with a smile. He enjoyed walking with Vera, they always got to talk about something interesting.

"That is a really good idea, I felt so uncomfortable opening the box on my own. It was obvious that it had been hidden for so long, I felt it best to leave opening it until you were around. I was going to ring you and then you turned up all of your own."

"I think you are probably right, someone is definitely trying to tell you something. How about if we open the box when we get home again? Where *is* the key? Have you still got it?"

"Oh Yes I do, it's the key that keeps moving about, I am sure I have told you about it before haven't I?"

"You might have done, but I can't have been paying much attention! Ok! Let's get going then!" Jimmy went to the hall to put his boots back on.

"Yes, let's do that," Vera agreed, "then let's buy some Battenberg cake in the post office, then we can make a pot of tea and open the box together."

The rain held off whilst they walked, but as soon as they had arrived back home the heavens opened with a vengeance. They joked about how lucky they had been as they hung up their anoraks and changed the walking boots to their indoor felt slippers. They were one of the many things the island was famous for.

It was cosy being indoors with the rain drumming on the roof and on the windows to windward. They lit candles and made tea and fed the stove a couple of logs, and together they sat down with the box at the dining table. Jimmy was really intrigued. It was indeed a very old box, and obviously it had been very important to the person who put it there. It just stood there in front of them. He lifted it gently; it seemed so tiny in his large hands, and studied carefully. He noticed that the string of wool was homespun; another sign that it was indeed very old.

" How can you tell its home spun? Vera asked

"Look!" he said, "the string is uneven, a sure sign it's spun on a spindle."

"What's that"

"It is a small stick with a hook at one end and a round stone at the other. It is rolled down over the thigh to twist the string, and from the hook the fine threads of wool are caught and twisted until it becomes a length of string, which is then wound round the bottom of the stick. It takes forever to spin like that. Only the wealthy had a proper spinning wheel that was worked with the foot. This gave a much more even spinning of the woollen string. Now of course it is all mechanised and you will never see uneven wool these days."

They ate the cake and drank the tea in silence.

"Oh, I'll need the key won't I?" Vera suddenly remembered and got up.

"Where is it Vera?"

"Just over there on the nail," she pointed and went to the kitchen and took the intricate little key down from the nail it had been hanging on since she moved in and found it in the wood shed. She showed it to Jimmy who was very impressed by the great skill with which it had been made. She gave it to him.

"Come to think of it! I am just remembering that one of the old lighthouse keepers, my uncle Adam, Adam MacCloud, the beekeeper, you know? He used to live in this croft, with his mum and his sister Anna, who was my mum. He died ohhh… it must be about 20 years ago, he had a terrible tummy ache for several days. On his deathbed he gave me a key on a string, just like this little tiny key. He said it belonged to Harbour View, and would I please return it to the croft. So I did. The new people had no idea what the key was for, and neither did I, so it was just hung on a nail in the kitchen, just like you have done. This key looks exactly like that key - I just wonder, could it possibly be the same one?"

"I suppose it could be, it would be strange if there were two such keys." Vera said.

"Right!" Jimmy put his mug down decisively, "Shall we open it? Let's see if the key fits."

Vera pulled it towards her and started to undo the bow on the string, it almost fell apart as soon as she started touching it. Bits of dust floated in the air from it, the box had been hidden for a very long time.

"This little key has kept appearing." Vera said as she fiddled with the woollen string. "I found it on the chopping block in the wood shed the very first day and brought it into the kitchen, I hung it on the nail over there," she turned and pointed at it, "but it never stays there. It is as if it has a life of its own, it appears all the time in different places, on the worktop, on the window sill, once I found it in the bathroom, it is as if it WANTS to be found, as if it is saying 'here I am'. And strangely enough every time I find it, it feels warm. You feel it!"

Jimmy picked it up.

"I see what you mean! It is indeed warm." Again Jimmy's wonderful thatched eyebrows flew up, surprised.

The little keyhole surround looked as if it was made of silver, it was tarnished, but could probably easily be polished up. There was a celtic pattern in the silver. The key fitted perfectly in the tiny lock and it opened easily with the slightest little click.

Vera lifted the lid carefully and with the same hesitation as you would a 'jack in the box'; being unsure what might appear.

It was full of neatly folded papers, and there was a pair of light blue baby-booties, and a small woollen wrap-around vest with the same platted woolly string to tie it on the side, as on the key and the box. All beautifully knitted of the finest home spun wool and on tiny needles. There was also an envelope with the inscription '*To my darling boy* ' written with pen and ink and with great care and attention in very old swirly handwriting.

Among the papers were a birth certificate and also a death certificate. There was a letter of congratulations on the birth of a baby boy, and two letters of condolences at the loss of a beloved husband. There were two months between the two occasions.

The distraught mother had written the letter in the envelope to the baby boy. Could the marks on the paper have been from tears? She tried to explain why she had made the difficult decision to adopt him away. Her pain was so tangible. Not only had she lost the love of her life and become a widow. But she had 3 small children including the two-month-old baby boy. It would be hard enough putting food on the table for 3 of them, and the new baby would never know or remember if he was given away now.

She had hardly got to know him yet, whereas the other two, a boy called Adam and a girl called Anna were a big part of her life. She asked that he would understand her difficult circumstance and begged for his forgiveness. The little boy's name was Arthur William MacCloud.

"Those are my fathers first names," said Vera astonished, the hairs on her arms stood on end.

"But his surname was Robinson. Wouldn't it be so strange if this was my dad? The birthday certainly fits." She shuddered, for some strange reason she had goose pimples.

"Maybe he was given the adoptive parents surname, but they kept his given names?" Jimmy suggested. "Is there any more information in the papers about the adoptive parents?"

They looked through the papers meticulously, and sure enough they found the name and address of the family he went to. It was indeed a Family Robinson who lived in Glasgow. They were a very well to do family who had come to hear of the little family's tragedy from their church minister who was a friend of the minister on the island.

They had written to Arthur's mother and thanked her for the wonderful little boy, 'that they, Praise the Lord! had been so fortunate to be given.' The letters were incredibly moving, and both Jimmy and Vera were moved to tears. When Vera became overcome with emotion, Jimmy gently put his arm reassuringly around her shoulders, and just held her without saying anything.

"So these were my Daddy's little booties." Vera said, picking them up. "Fancy he wore these. I am so sorry he never knew of the box and that he never got the letter. Do you really think it was him, or am I imagining things? Am I making things up?

"No!" said Jimmy, "I think there is a very good chance this is your dad. Did he know that he was adopted?"

"Oh yes, he knew that, because he told us so. But I find it strange that he never tried to find his roots. We've actually never been to Glasgow to visit his parents, I wonder what happened to them?"

"Maybe they died, or maybe it just wasn't necessary for him to find his roots. Maybe he was extremely happy where he was. He was a man, Vera." Jimmy said convincingly.

"And what do you mean with that? " Surprised she looked up at him.

And Jimmy continued,

"Do you know the old saying? You have a girl, you have her for life; you have a boy until he finds a wife. Some boys and men don't have the same need to find their roots. When the cord is cut, it's cut. And that is how it is. We don't look back, we look forward. Did you ever read the book 'Men are from Mars and women are from Venus'?"

She shook her head,

"What is it about?"

"It just explains a lot of the differences between men and women. I have it at home, you can borrow it if you like." He smiled at her. This was an awful lot to take in all at once.

"How about if I put the kettle on for another cuppa? He said. " And I do think we need another piece of cake too don't we?"

"Yes please, what a good idea." She stayed at the table looking at all the papers once more.

So Adam was her father's older brother and Anna his older sister and she was also Jimmy's mum. This was why the little old lady had come to see her. She must have been Vera's Grandmother, and Vera's dad had actually been born in this very house. She found it all very hard to believe. The most likely reason that she felt so at home here, was because her roots *were* here. This was why it had all seemed so familiar.

She had indeed come home, when she returned to the island. It had been so comforting to share all this with Jimmy. She left the papers on the table and the two of them sat on the sofa and chatted about all they had found out.

Arthur's father, Vera's grandfather, had been a fisherman, they gathered from the death certificate. He had drowned when his boat had been smashed on the rocks in a storm. This they read in the newspaper cutting. And Jimmy could also add memories about it that his mother and Grandmother had told him.

"That would have been long before the lighthouse and the foghorn had been installed. Maybe now you will feel better when you hear the foghorn and know that it will keep someone else safe?"

She nodded, confirming that that was precisely her thoughts. They sat in silence for a little while. When Jimmy suddenly sat upright with a jolt and said,

"This means that your father is my mother's little brother! And that means that we are related... We're actually cousins."

They looked at each other without saying anything for a while-and then they just burst out laughing, and hugged each other.

"This is unbelievable! Maybe my dad did bring us here when I was very small? Maybe that is why it feels so right? So it was my grandmother, who came to see me last night! And she is the one who has been moving the key about, all the time."

I really think we should pay a visit to the cemetery by the church, they are all there, grandma and grandpa, my mum and dad, and Adam. I do go there on their birthdays, and on the anniversary of their deaths. Let's go tomorrow shall we? If the weather is ok that is? I think a visit to a cemetery is best done on a sunny day, don't you?"

Vera couldn't agree more. She had found it very difficult, when she went to Martin's grave to tell him that she was moving to Scotland. Not knowing when she would be able to come back. Friends had promised to tend to the grave when they were visiting their own relatives' graves.

It had been a very emotional day, but it had also laid some ghosts to rest. Literally. She didn't think there would be any more night visits or disturbing dreams from now on. And the key would stay in the lock where it belonged. They tied a ribbon on it that also surrounded the box so the two could never be parted again.

It felt good to have shared it all with Jimmy and together they decided not to put the box back where Vera's grandmother had put it all those years ago; back under the loose floorboard in the cupboard upstairs. From now on it would have pride of place on the mantelpiece. Before Jimmy left they decided to speak on the phone tomorrow about the possibility of paying a visit to the churchyard so he could show Vera her ancestors' graves.

The next day the sun was shining from a cloudless sky, and Jimmy rang to say that as the forecast was good, he would come over with Sirius and they could go to the graveyard and visit the grave. Vera went to her meadow and made a little posy of the few flowers that were blooming.

It was very emotional to visit the graves. All the headstones had lichen and moss on them. They were all there, Vera and her husband, Adam, and Anna and her husband. It was strange but very emotional for Vera to be standing at her ancestor's graves. These were people that she felt close to and yet had never known.

They were both quiet, each in their own thoughts, and after a while they entered the church. The sun was illuminating the huge stained glass windows. The beams that shone through the plain glass areas, made strong rays into the room, and in them dust particles could be seen dancing. They lit some candles and sat down and thought privately about their ancestors.

The priest came in preparing for evensong and slowly other parishioners came too and it felt good to be surrounded by others. The little service was uplifting and they wandered back to Harbour View. As it was Vera's first visit to the church, she shook hands with the priest at the door, and he welcomed her warmly to the island. She thought he was a quietly spoken, thoughtful and intelligent man, with a firm handshake and very kind eyes. She warmed to him instantly.

Because dusk had already settled by the time they arrived Jimmy stayed the night, and they shared a lovely meal together celebrating that they were cousins, and talked about how lucky they were that they had found each other.

Now it all seemed to fit like a perfect puzzle, perhaps her dad had brought her here when she was a little girl? And that's the reason it all seemed so familiar. How wonderful to find a long lost cousin, and this explained why she felt so good in Jimmy's company too. She *had* known him all her life-she just didn't know it.

# 37

The bees arrived in a small case early in June. Vera had bought a mated Aeolian Queen and she came with her little entourage of worker bees in a small box. She had been so excited about their arrival. Vera put them in a nucleus box with some home made sugar syrup feed, and placed the hive next to the meadow of bee-friendly flowers that she had prepared and sown and which was now in full bloom at the bottom of the garden. The queen quickly started laying eggs, and was very productive.

The bees had plenty of room when she moved them over into a proper brood chamber a month later. She had even been able to fit two supers for honey storage on top of the queen excluder. They were busy capping the honey in August and she was very pleased with the prospect of being able to harvest some honey already this year. She was exhilarated when she finally took some of the honey off, leaving a large amount for the bees for the winter and ended up with 12 jars of gorgeous golden runny-honey.

She was wondering how quickly it would set, which of course depended on the amount of sugar the honey contained. The better the honey the quicker it would set. The new group of potential beekeepers were pleased to have a jar each, and rumours quickly went round the island how good the honey was.

The hive at the lighthouse had also worked hard, and she had been able to take honey off there too, but this was of course without Jimmy's help. That honey was given to the post office to sell so as many islanders as possible had the opportunity to have some Island of Strathsay honey. Once that hive had been wintered, she would tape up the entrance and the new beekeeper group would help to move the hive, who was going to be the new owner had not been decided yet.

The summer also brought lots of visitors and she was grateful for the spare room upstairs. Her son Michael and his partner Helen had been for a week at the end of

June. They had celebrated the summer solstice by getting engaged!

It was a fantastic evening and it hardly got dark all night. They sat outside with candles until long after midnight. Helens beautiful ring glittered in the candlelight. The youngsters had been so happy, looking at each other, holding hands, and with smiles that never seemed to leave their faces. Vera had been so pleased they had chosen to get engaged whilst visiting her.

Lisa and her husband came for a week to go walking and enjoy the island. There were some cruises in the summer, to look at seals and birds, which they went on, on the days Vera worked. Lisa was very interested to hear of the nursing set up on the island. She called it a jewel in the crown service, which it really was.

The vegetable garden was a great joy and a huge success, and she was able to pick raspberries and black currants, from which she made jams and jellies. So many that she was able to sell some at the post office.

The potatoes were delicious, and so were the climbing green beans,and she feasted on them almost daily. She was able to sell some to the shop, and got many remarks from some of the islanders about how industrious she was.

# 38

Very early one summer morning she noticed that something was interfering with the way the sunlight usually glittered on the water. Suddenly she heard a big splash followed by a strange clunking and rattling noise, which made her sit up in her bed.

Much to her surprise a sailing boat had arrived in 'her' little bay. It was the noise of the anchor being laid out on the seabed that she could hear. The heavy chain wriggled out over the front of the boat from the anchor locker, as the boat slowly moved backwards. She sat in bed and watched the skipper working on the boat. She looked at the time; it was only 5.17 in the morning, *'just a tad too early to start the day for me,'* she thought. Vera reckoned that the skipper must have sailed all night, '*I hope he doesn't try to come ashore on "my" beach, he won't know where all the birds are nesting,*' Vera thought anxiously.

She decided to get up and keep an eye on what the sailor did, as she would have to warn him about getting ashore just there. She did know of another safe place that she could guide him to. Having laid the anchor, and tested that it was biting, he went below, and then there was no further sign of him, nor any noises from the boat. The boat just bobbed quietly in the morning sun, on the small ripples of waves that came ashore on the still morning.

*I think he has gone to bed, if he was moving about I am sure it would disturb the water around the boat. I'll go and put the kettle on and make a cup of tea.* She brought the tea and her binoculars back into the bedroom and sat in the warm bed and enjoyed the new view-it was a beautiful big yacht. She imagined that there was more than the skipper on board. But if that was the case, why had nobody come to help him drop the anchor.

She wondered while sipping her tea. *I think it must be a live on board boat, and maybe they have come a long way.* She was looking at all the gear tied on to the foredeck. There was a red kayak, and a bicycle, and several big red and yellow plastic jerry cans, securely tied on. There was also a wind generator whizzing around at the stern of the boat.

She had drunk her tea and as all was quiet on the boat so she decided to get up. She got washed and dressed and put the kettle on again to make some breakfast. She let the chickens out of the coop, the bees were already flying, she acknowledged with a little smile. She was rewarded with two freshly laid eggs-she would have one of them for breakfast.

She had a strange bubbly happy feeling that today would be a very special day.

Later in the morning she heard noises from the boat again, the skipper was back up on the deck. Vera got the binoculars out and looked at what he was doing. He was trying to get his rubber dinghy into the water. 'He is going to try to row ashore-he really mustn't come ashore right here-I'll go down and warn him.'

As soon as Vera walked out of the little gate and crossed the track, the skipper saw her and waved. Vera waved back and lifted both arms, as if she pressed the flat hands against a pane of glass, to say stop! Then she pointed to the right with her right arm outstretched, as she waved the left hand in a scooping circle, saying "Come over there."

She walked along the track, so she could get to the safe place herself to show him where to get ashore. He rowed fast and with surprising strength. His blond curls were moving, as he pulled hard on the oars. He must be of Viking descent with a body like that. He was not bad looking either, she noticed as he came nearer. She held on to the dinghy as he stepped ashore.

"Good morning and welcome to Strathsay." She greeted him with a smile. He jumped out of the boat, in well worn shorts-the ragged leftovers of what had once been jeans and bare feet. He stretched out his hand-"Sven!" and she replied "Vera!" The greeting was simple, but warm. The handshake took her by surprise though, it was very firm and his hand was warm and dry, calloused from a lot of rowing and pulling in sheets. He looked directly into her eyes-with such an intensity, that she had to look away.

"Thank you for guiding me ashore-what was all that waving about?"

"There are nesting birds on the shore and it is an especially protected area. I saw you arrive early this morning and was worried that you would come to the shore, so I have kept an eye on you. It was a very early arrival, have you come from far away?" They chatted and helped each other bringing the boat high up above the tideline on the beach and he then tied the painter to a large stone.

"Yes I have been island hopping around Britain since I retired in May last year. I got caught in the strong currents yesterday afternoon. Their strength rather surprised me, and it took me a lot longer than I had anticipated, hence the late arrival. Fortunately I found this lovely little quiet bay, dropped the anchor so I could get a few hours badly needed shut-eye. I do need some provisions though, and it said in my information that Strathsay has both a post office and a shop."

"We sure do, we even have an excellent butcher too. But it's a 20-minute walk from here. Why don't you moore at the jetty? That will be a lot easier for you if you need a lot of things."

"That is a good idea! I didn't tie up there when I arrived, as I needed to sleep, and as there is quite a tide here, I would need to keep adjusting the mooring warps, so it was much better to just drop the anchor in the bay."

"Yes I heard it –it made quite a clattering noise!"

"Sorry! Noise travels so easily over the water."

"Have you had breakfast? I can offer you a freshly laid egg and some tea, and you are welcome to have a shower too." Vera was keen to hear more about his exciting travels; and he sure looked like he could do with a shower.

"I would love both, if I am not inconveniencing you. Do you sail? It would be handy with a hand to tie up at the jetty, if you have the time."

"I have never been on a sailing boat, so I am not sure I'll be any help at all."

"No worries-if you are keen. I'll tell you exactly what to do-extra hands are extra hands and they are always welcome."

They made their way up to Harbour View. Sven was in awe of the beauty of the island.

"Doesn't it just look so different from ashore? It is amazing what a difference a few metres height makes. You actually don't sound Scottish, so what brought you here?"

"Well that is in fact a very long story, but basically I am the island's new beekeeper. I arrived in March, I have come to set up new bee hives and make sure the bees survive the winter."

She noticed his white teeth as he smiled broadly.

"What a fantastic job! I have always been interested in beekeeping, but I have never come across a beekeeper. You will have to tell me more."

They walked up to the house, he commented on the solar panels, and said that he too had just the one on board. A great help when sailing long distances.

Vera showed him the bathroom and gave him a towel and whilst he showered, she made breakfast. She could hear him humming in the bathroom, there was such an easy going air around him.

He was easy to talk to and their conversation flowed easily as he helped get breakfast ready. Sitting at the table, he suddenly put his head in his hands. Vera noticed that he got very pale.

"Are you ok?" Vera was immediately concerned, sudden pallor like this could be heart trouble. Automatically she reached for his wrist, to check his pulse.

"Whoahh!" he exclaimed-"I think I'm getting land sick." He got up and started moving about.

"What is that?"

"Well if you have been moving about on a boat for a long time and then come ashore and sit still, you can experience the same feeling of seasickness that you can get when you first start sailing. I'll be ok, I just need to keep moving about- I hope you don't mind me having breakfast standing up?"

"No of course not-you just do what feels right for you."

After breakfast she showed him the beehive and the chickens.

"You have a great place here Vera, what a pearl you have found. I think you have been a very brave lady to move up here, but I think it was the right decision. I sense that you have settled well and are very happy here."

"Yes, I am very content. It was difficult to downsize and say goodbye to many things that I held dear, but strangely it has also been very liberating.

"I know exactly what you mean, I sold everything to buy this boat, and it was the best thing I have ever done. I am as free as the bird I can go or stay and do exactly as I feel like. You are exactly right, it is liberating."

Later he rowed them back out to the boat. With some degree of difficulty she managed to climb on board from the bobbing rubber dinghy. He noticed the struggle and with no hesitation what-so-ever he gave her but a push, to help her up.

"I hope you didn't mind a helping hand, did you?" he laughed. Vera smiled back over her shoulder as she stepped on board-it was too late to mind if she had. She was impressed with his easy approach to life, it was often easier to get away with an apology than ask for permission.

Then they tied the dinghy onto the boat and towed it behind as they motored gently across the bay to the jetty. Sven told her how to steer and hold the course on the compass, before he went forwards to prepare the mooring warps and attached the fenders.

It was a calm day, the sea was flat, the sun was shining, and Vera was beginning to enjoy steering the boat. Suddenly a huge wave came silently across the quiet water. None of them noticed, as Vera had her eyes on the jetty and Sven was concentrating on the work in hand, they didn't realise the imminent danger. The boat was suddenly hit by the unexpected huge swell. In Vera's inexperienced hands the boat broached, and Sven immediately lost his balance and went straight overboard.

"Throttle in neutral!" He managed to shout before he hit the water.

Vera automatically turned the wheel to steer away from him, thinking… *throttle throttle, which one is the throttle?* She looked around, and noticed the silver handle on the column in front of the wheel that the compass was mounted on. It was pointing slightly forwards, she pulled it towards her, and it clicked into neutral.

"Well done!" shouted Sven, but the boat didn't stop, the tide was taking it.

"What shall I do now?" Vera was desperately frightened, she could hear her pulse in her ears, and her chest felt too small for the hammering heart.

"Calm down! You can do this! Just follow my instructions. Press the button on the throttle and move it gently forwards and then keep steering left and go round in a big circle. As she went past him the first time, he told her to flip the Dan-buoy off the hook at the stern. Then she could better keep an eye on where he was, as the flag on it would be much easier to see. It is very difficult to see a person in the water, especially without an aid, you can so easily lose sight of the casualty. As she approached him the second time he shouted,

"Just slowly, slowly, come towards me, I will try to swim towards the back of the boat. Put the throttle in neutral before you get to me and try to glide towards me."

Vera tried a few times, going round in big circles. It felt very wrong going away from him, and it was really difficult to keep an eye on him. She was grateful that she had been able to drop the buoy with the flag. He swam to the buoy and held on to the rope attached to it. As she glided nearer, he was able to pull himself towards the boat, and eventually got to the stern and could get back on board, once he was sure the propeller had stopped.

The water in north Scotland is never warm, not even in the summer, and Sven was really cold after his involuntary swim. His lips were blue and he was shivering like Vera had only ever seen desperately ill patients shiver. He quickly got changed and put some warm clothes on and together they sailed over to the jetty, this time with Sven on the helm. Once safely moored, he put the kettle on and made them a hot chocolate with a good glug of rum.

"You did so well Vera! Anyone would have panicked, but you just kept cool and followed my instructions. I am really proud of the way you handled this situation. I reckon it was the wash from a submarine, there are lots of them up here and they do create a large swell. It's not your fault at all."

He put his arms around her and hugged her closely. Vera could feel her diaphragm muscles contract, and tears burned behind her eyelids, and suddenly she sobbed. Sven didn't say anything; words weren't necessary. He just held her, until eventually the sobbing stopped.

"I'm sorry! I didn't mean to cry. It was just so scary. I had no idea what to do. You could have drowned. I have never been in such an out- of- control situation. I have been in many scary situations at work, but never in one like this. It felt so scary. I think I have put my feet on a boat for both the first and the last time in a single day."

"Oh please don't say that Vera, I would really like to sail more with you. You mustn't give up at the first hurdle. You did extremely well."

For quite a while they sat quietly sipping their warm restoring drink, and then they went to the shop. Sven was introduced to the Morrison family, who by now were firm friends of Vera's. Vera helped to bring the provisions to the boat and also helped to stove them away. There was order everywhere.

Sven had plans for sailing on to see other places, hence the topping up of his provisions.

"But I will be back, Vera, I promise. And then I hope that you will come sailing with me, there are some lovely islands I would like to show you!"

Vera hesitated and said that she would have to talk to Beth about having some holiday, as she was working in the surgery two mornings a week.

"Maybe you can let me know, when you are thinking of coming back, then I might be able to get some time off. But honestly I don't mind if it is in a little while, as I really don't feel like sailing just now."

"Well I recommend that you get back on the horse as fast as possible, but I do also understand that this has been a very scary experience for you. I will let you know when I am thinking of returning. I think some quiet sailing at the end of the summer would be lovely. Please think about it."

Sven walked her back up to Harbour View, and they said goodbye, both being keen to meet again later in the summer. Then time would tell whether Vera would be keen to go sailing again.

# 39

The delivery man from John Lewis came later in July with his wife and two children and spent a whole week bird watching and walking. They had been self catering at Harbour View, and meanwhile Vera stayed in the spare room at the Doctor's House with Beth and she was able to help every day at the surgery. With countless visitors to the island the surgery had been open every day, and there had been no end of the variety of complaints. Some had forgotten their medication, there was a suspected heart attack, burst blisters on sore walkers feet and different severity of cuts and sprains. Vera didn't have to come to the surgery every day, but was on standby if Beth got called away or got really busy, but she enjoyed it and was there most days.

The post office family also had family visiting in July and asked if two of the children could possibly borrow the spare room at Vera's. That went well, as they only turned up to sleep and they went back home on their bikes as soon as they woke up in the morning, so they were no trouble at all,

Ruth and Dick had been twice during the summer and they had all had a lovely time together. Jimmy had invited them all to see the lighthouse, a visit the youngsters had found most interesting. He had been in his element explaining how the lighthouse worked and telling them what it was like to work as a lighthouse keeper. He did guided tours for tourists, which added a little income for him too, so he was well rehearsed, and his wealth of knowledge seemed like a bottomless pit.

She had spent the summer tending the kitchen garden which had been a great joy too. It had kept her very busy, not just with the work she had to do in it, but she also appreciated the fantastic bonus of being able to harvest and process the rich pickings.

She had a good crop of beetroot, which she had pickled in Kilner jars. She had so much that she had sold some to the shop. She had been picking loads of green beans too, and ate them every single day. They were delicious, and she had been able to put some in the freezer for the winter. Some had also been sold to the shop. The new potatoes had been absolutely delicious, and she had enjoyed digging them up, scrubbing them and putting them straight into the boiling water for dinner. "You really can't beat the taste of newly dug up potatoes with ice-cold salty butter", she could hear Grannie's voice again.

The summer birds had been frequent visitors at the bird table, and she had been out for many long walks, always with the binoculars round her neck and her notebook in her pocket. She enjoyed keeping a record of what she saw and heard around her. All her little contributions to the magazine had been very popular. The editor forwarded some of the letters she had received from some readers. They had been so encouraging. Especially she enjoyed reading those from housebound seniors who had so appreciated her descriptions of the nature around her. So even from here, on this small island she was able to bring joy to others.

She had walked with Simon up to the lighthouse on several occasions; Jimmy had never had the luxury of having a family. He so enjoyed Simon's company and they always had such a great time together. He would have made a great dad. Little Rosie thrived and grew, and you wouldn't really know now that she had been born so prematurely. She was passing all her milestones with fine marks.

Vera started painting again, and soon had quite a little collection of pictures, which she was selling both at the teashop on the cliffs and at the post office. Hamish had suggested that she gave some to the art and craft shop on the mainland, for them to sell and whet the tourists appetite to visit Strathsay.

Her flapjacks had, as predicted by Mr Morrison on that very first day, been a fantastic success, and now that she could even look forward to putting some honey in them they would surely be even more sought after. So all in all she could not complain.

## 40

In August the heather bloomed and the hills were an unbelievable sight of deep purple. She couldn't wait to take some of the heather honey off the hives kept up there-heather honey being the best of the best. Especially if it was creamed. A special method of stirring the honey daily to prevent it from setting, by breaking the sugars, until it eventually just becomes like cream.

A few days into the month she had a phone call from Mrs M to say that Sven had rung from another island to check Vera's phone number, as the number he had didn't work. He was so apologetic and asked if Mrs M would let Vera know that he would be arriving in a couple of days time.

*'That is actually great, then he can help with the honey making-I think he will enjoy that.*

When Sven then rang to say that he was on the jetty and would she be interested in sailing with him. She had already been speaking to Beth about the possibility of a few days off, if Sven should return, which Beth of course had agreed to. Her fear had not subsided, and she didn't really fancy going sailing with him. Vera had so hoped to hear from him, and was deeply disappointed that she didn't-So when he eventually did ring, she was not exactly over-joyed. Well she was pleased, but she didn't let on. She was rather reserved, polite but reserved.

"Hey Vera, what's up? You don't sound happy?"

"Well I had rather hoped to hear from you whilst you were gone, and to be honest I am disappointed that you haven't tried to ring me."

"I tried to ring you, but I must have written the number down wrongly, I am terribly dyslexic, so not until I could get in touch with the post office and get your number from Mrs M- I'm so sorry I couldn't get in touch with you-but here I am! Are you busy? Fancy coming down? Or would you rather I come up to you?"

"I'll come down, you will only get landsick if you come up here."

She hadn't realised how happy it made her to know that she would be seeing him again, and she had to make herself walk at an appropriate speed, even though her heart wanted her to run.

He stood on the quay with his hand to his brow, watching out for her, and as soon as he saw her he started running towards her. Vera let go too and ran towards him and they met in a big embrace.
He lifted her and swung her round, hugging her tightly,

"Oh my God Vera, how I've missed you." He gently put her down again and looked into her eyes, and then kissed her. A small, but ever so tender kiss on her cheek.

She leant into his body, and let him embrace her. Aww this felt so good, she had certainly also missed him, more than she cared to admit.

"Come on board Vera!" Sven was nimble and was quickly on board and gave her a hand to step over the guard-rails. Going down below, it smelt so comforting and homely, and she remembered the lovely hot chocolate they had enjoyed, the last time she was on board. And how he had comforted her when she cried.

"What can I offer you m'lady? I have to be honest with you Vera, I have put a bottle of champagne in the fridge-I've been so excited about seeing you again-what do you say? Shall we celebrate with some bubbles?"

"The last time I had bubbles was when I decided to take on this exciting challenge of moving up here-so why not! Champagne sounds great! Thank you very much. Are we sitting down here or in the cockpit?"

"I actually thought it would be nice if we sailed over to your bay and dropped the anchor. It's going to be a beautiful summer night with clear skies. Then we can sit in the cockpit and watch the stars. What do you think?"

*'Sounds like he has planned a rather nice evening'* Vera thought to herself.

"That sounds really nice, Sven. Let's do that." Vera was in no doubt that some of the islanders would have noticed her getting onboard, and she was not going to let them have the benefit of having something to gossip about, if they saw her sitting in the cockpit drinking Champagne.

She went back up in the cockpit, Sven cast off and sailed them back to the little bay. This gave Vera the time to think about the evening ahead and to think about how she felt about seeing Sven again. Was she ready for romance? It had been so very nice to see him again, but no she was not ready, Martin was still the man in her life. But she so appreciated the very warm friendship.

Sven dropped the anchor and peace settled on board as soon as he turned the engine off. It was so quiet. All she could hear was the gentle lapping of little waves against the hull, and the curlews on the shore.

Sven went down below and came up with the champagne and some snacks.

"So how do you feel about coming for a sail with me, now that you are onboard again?"

Vera had to admit that the mere thought filled her with anxiety..

"I'm ok sitting here, whilst we are at anchor, but just sailing across from the jetty I could feel how anxious I was getting. I am sorry to let you down, Sven. Also as you can see the heather is in full bloom and shortly we shall have to take the honey off the hives up there and then winter them. If that is something you will be interested in you will be more than welcome to join in."

"That sounds really great. I would love to help with that, when is it going to be?"

"Not before later this month, what are your sailing plans?"

"I am hoping to take part in the ARC in November…"

"Sorry I don't know what that is?" Vera interrupted before he got any further.

"It's a group of yachts sailing across the Atlantic from the Canary Islands to the Caribbean, so I could really do with some crew-ie you!" Sven laughed, tongue in cheek.

"I'm really sorry to let you down Sven, but I don't think a huge journey is for me. I have only recently moved here and I am still settling in. But I do appreciate being asked."

Sven popped the cork and poured the wine, the sun sparkled in the bubbles that rose to the surface, in fine lines from the bottom of the glass.

"This island is so beautiful and to view it through a glass of bubbles makes it look even more inviting and fantastic. Just look at that colour on the hills, isn't it astonishing?" Vera leaned back and relaxed.

There was so much on the island that she was grateful for and enjoyed and now that she had put her cards on the table, she could lean back and just enjoy his company. She would certainly enjoy the evening with him. They had a great friendship in the making, but they were both going their own ways, and there was no doubt, she thought, that he would swing by the island when he returned from the trip across the atlantic.

The stars were truly amazing and they enjoyed the evening sitting in the cockpit. He had his arm around her shoulders and she leaned into his warm comforting body.

She wanted these special moments to never end. That was what her heart told her, but her very sensible mind had a different agenda. There was a bit of a battle going on between the two. Sensible Vera against all the temptations presented to her won and they had a wonderful peaceful evening together. Sven cooked a lovely meal for them, which they ate on their lap in the cockpit with a million stars above them.

"I'll just go down and put the kettle on. As we have shared a bottle of bubbles, are you happy to stay onboard for the night? I can soon fix you a bed to sleep on?"

Vera was relaxed and drowsy, and didn't feel like the evening should come to an end, so said yes thank you to the kind offer. Sven rummaged about whilst the kettle came to boil and brought her tea up. Once that was drunk, they settled for the night. Peaceful and quietly they drifted off after a lovely evening together.

After breakfast Sven rowed her ashore and walked her home. See you around, they said when they hugged goodbye. Time would tell if this was going to be more than a friendship, but at the moment it felt right to leave it like that.

# 41

The first six months had been busy and full of joy, but autumn was coming. She wintered the bees in September. The queen excluder was removed, enabling the cluster to move freely over the honey stores, and a mouse guard was placed in front of the entrance. This was to enable the bees to exit for a cleansing-flight on sunny days. From experience she had learnt, that you do not hang out your washing on the first sunny day after a run of rainy days in winter-as that would for sure be a cleansing-flight day for the bees and your washing would show the signs, with many a little yellow spot on the washing. She asked Jimmy if he would like to take part in making this year's Christmas cake.

"You are certainly out early Vera, it's only September, but yes I would love to take part in that."

Vera ordered all the ingredients, and Mrs M commented that she was glad to have such an organised customer, because she was sure others would not be far behind Vera in making theirs so now she could order all the ingredients in bulk.

They made and baked the Christmas cake together, and they both made a wish as they stirred it, not telling what it was! It baked for hours in the simmering oven in the AGA and once it was cooled it was then put in a tin. It had had a good bit of whisky poured over it and then it was left in the cool shed for weeks to soak it all up and mature. It had to have a little feed of whisky now and again, and they helped each other to remember to do it.

It was the light icy-blue sky and the chill in the wind that first gave the change in the weather away; ever so faint at first, but definitely there. But she was made aware for sure, that winter was knocking on the door, when Mrs M rang to advise it was time to order firewood and peat and to book in the chimney sweep. The weather changes were ever so gentle at first. The days had begun to shorten at the summer solstice, un-noticeably at first but at the September equinox the nights were definitely drawing in. The temperature dropped at night with the clear and starry skies. Once the clocks had been put back at the end of October, the days became very short indeed.

Then it was Halloween too. The children had carved pumpkins with scary faces, and made them into lanterns. They were everywhere, outside the post office and at the school gate they were lined up on the wall of the playground and also she saw them in many windows. A big halloween party was held at the village hall, and it was great fun. The children were dressed up as ghouls and ghosts, and there had been all sorts of pumpkin related foods.Vera thought the best had been the soup. She had added pumpkin mash to her amazing homemade rolls, but she was not best pleased with the result, even though others were very complimentary about them.

The last day of the month had been a lovely bright but very windy day. The strong westerly winds were again sweeping in over the island and huge waves were now crashing against the rocky shoreline with a thunderous rumble that could be heard all over the island. She went out to open the coop, and walked past by the bees. The beehive was fairly quiet, just one or two little ones dared to venture out, a sure sign that rain was on the way. She had wintered them in early September, but it was good to see the odd bee sneaking out through the mouse guard for a little nose-about.

The fine salty sea spray was carried all over the island. If you went outside you could taste it when licking your lips, and you could also feel it in your hair, which quickly became stiff and unruly.

The windows bore the unmistakable evidence too. They looked disgracefully dirty, but there was absolutely no point in cleaning them whilst the wind was so strong.

It had been one of those days that it was really great to be outside-for a while-and then even nicer to get back inside to the warm wood stove. Today she had been chopping and stacking wood, a load of logs had been delivered and had to be stacked neatly away in the woodshed for the winter. It had been great fun but also quite exhausting, so when she returned from the afternoon's halloween party at the village hall she had retired to bed after a long warm bath. Soothing those hard worked muscles. She was well aware that she would be aching all over tomorrow.

## 42

She made sure she had plenty of firewood in the shed, including some big bits that Dick could have some fun splitting when he next came visiting! Mrs M had alerted her to the fact that it was time to order firewood and have the chimneys swept in August/ September. So she had put in an order for a load of logs and also some peat turfs, as they had been so marvellous during the chilly nights when she had first arrived in March.

So slowly but surely she prepared for the long winter evenings as the nights drew in. She ordered t-lights and candles from the mainland, and bought books on Amazon. She had learnt to live with the Aga and the wood burners, and the new way of life had become easy, and very satisfying.

She had made great friends especially with Jimmy and of course the little family round the headland. Simon would often pop in on his way home from school, with either mum or dad, and they would often stop for a cup of tea and a chat. Sometimes he would stay and she would walk him home later, but now the evenings were dark, they walked straight home and had a chat on the way if Vera fetched him from school, which she sometimes did.

Ruth and Dick announced their arrival for Christmas and when Michael heard that, he and Helen decided they would like to come too. When she spoke to Jimmy about his plans for Christmas and the New Year, and discovered that he didn't have any, she invited him too. He had not made a lot out of the so-called festive season himself, since he had been alone in the lighthouse. Before when there had been three of them it had been quite a jolly day, as each had brought their own special Christmas traditions and treats to the table.

There were a lot of preparations to do to make it a special Christmas for everyone, but Vera and Jimmy helped each other on many occasions. They had walked to the forest together and found "their" Christmas tree, they had put a ribbon on it and reserved it. They bought decorations on the internet; and to their delight found that they liked exactly the same things.

Time and time again it felt as if they had known one another for years. They just enjoyed the ease with which their friendship slowly developed. It was the care for each other that pleased Vera so much.

It thrilled her that he had paid attention to the little things she liked. For example, that she loved watching songs of praise on a Sunday afternoon in the winter whilst enjoying a glass of wine.

He had also noticed that she loved a cup of tea in bed first thing in the morning and last thing at night too. Whenever he stayed over, he slept upstairs and he always respected her privacy, and would always be one step ahead to please her. He would knock in the morning with a cup of tea, and sit on her bed and drink his own after putting wood in the stove, so the rooms would be lovely and warm for her to get up to.

The week before Christmas they decorated the house, and made it all pretty with holly sprigs and the freshly cut tree which stood beautifully in the corner of the room. It smelled amazing. The cake was iced and decorated, and looked very appetising, with sprigs of holly and a few red berries and a beautiful golden ribbon all the way around it.

At the winter solstice on the 21 of December a colourful postcard arrived from Antigua in the Caribbean, saying "I have arrived safely after a great sail, and will tell you all about it when we meet again. Love from Sven xx" Vera put it on the mantelpiece, together with the other christmas cards that had arrived to wish her a wonderful christmas and new year. It was good to know that he was safely on the other side of the atlantic.

There was great anticipation of the Christmas guests' arrival, and she was so pleased to have plenty of cold storage available in the shed for all the necessary food for all of them. She had ordered a big smoked leg of ham as well as the turkey, and had plenty of flour to make homemade rolls as and when necessary. They all arrived together on the last ferry before christmas, and Hamish kindly offered to drive them up to Harbour View with all their luggage.

Unbeknown to Ruth, Dick had asked Vera for Ruth's hand in marriage and Vera had kept it a secret apart from sharing the good news with Jimmy. So on Christmas Eve when they were all gathered ready for a pre-dinner drink, Jimmy made and excuse to go outside, Sirius lifted his head, to see what was going on, but stayed on the blanket near the stove, at the same time Vera left the table and returned with a tray with 6 champagne glasses.

"Hey what's this now?" exclaimed Ruth surprised, then Jimmy came in with a bottle of champagne, which had been chilling outside and Dick smiled and tapped his finger on the side of his nose, knowingly, but wondered if Ruth had found out about his plan to propose to her. There were question marks in every face? Jimmy was the first to ping on his glass,

"I would like to thank you all for being here, and for making me so very welcome in your - in my family. A family I didn't even know I had! And welcome home to Strathsay all of you. Cheers! And a very merry Christmas to you all." He lifted his glass, ready for it to be filled for the toast.

"Just a moment," Dick rose to his feet.

"I have something I would like to say too! First of all I would like to thank Vera for ordering Solar panels for Harbour View. Without this order Ruth and I would not have met, and I have to say this year has been so amazing in so many ways. I am so grateful for this new family. You have all made me so welcome, that I would like to make this permanent."

Then without any further ado he went down on one knee and said,

"Ruth! Will you marry me?" Before she could answer he held out a beautiful diamond ring. She smiled, looked at Vera, who nodded with tears in her eyes, and then said,

"Yes I will Dick!" He then placed the ring on her finger. She looked at it, he had chosen it so well, the diamond was placed *in* the ring so it was smooth and flat and enabled her to wear her surgical gloves over it.

"Well if this doesn't call for celebrations I don't know," said Michael and grabbed the champagne bottle and popped the cork and poured the sparkling bubbly wine into the awaiting glasses and said, "Just before you drink, Helen and I would like to say that we have reason to celebrate too, as we are expecting a baby in July!" Then they all toasted and cheered and the newly engaged couple kissed, Vera and Jimmy hugged. Helen very sensibly only took just a small sip of her glass and passed it to Michael, who was more than happy to drink both glasses.

Then they sat down at the festive dinner table. The tree glittered and sparkled in the corner. What an unforgettable Christmas Eve!

"What an amazing year it has been, thanks to everyone who has supported me in this new adventure, and here's to many more."

Vera lifted her glass,

"Cheers everybody! Thank you all for coming and celebrating Christmas here!"

They all lifted their glasses again and toasted each other,

"And here's to many more happy hours in Harbour View. A big thank you to this wonderful island, that has made all of us so welcome and very happy. Merry Christmas!"

What would the next year bring?

## THANK YOU

I would like to thank Betinna Hansen from New York and Karen Grothe Moeller who have been invaluable in their help. I also want to thank Reverend Donald McCorkindale for the lovely photograph for the front cover. Thank you to Charlie at Magic Daisy Publishing for making my dream a reality.

## ABOUT THE AUTHOR

Joanna Nightingale was born in Denmark in 1954. She married her English husband in 1980, shortly after qualifying as a midwife. They moved to England in 1982 with their new-born daughter. They have three daughters and 5 grandchildren. She joined the creative writing group in the local U3A ten years ago, and is still an active member.

## ABOUT MAGIC DAISY PUBLISHING

Magic Daisy Publishing is an independent imprint which supports authors and illustrators who are interested in becoming published writers.

We'd love you to check out our website:

**www.magicdaisypublishing.co.uk**

You can also find us on Facebook where we have more information about our authors, illustrators and future competitions.

**www.facebook.com/magicdaisypublishing**

Thank you for your interest in Magic Daisy Publishing!

MAGIC DAISY
*Publishing*

Printed in Great Britain
by Amazon